This book is dedicated to my own Mr Smith, Geoffrey, who walked into my life at just the right time. Though this dedication wouldn't be complete without thanking my daughter, Matiesha, and my boys, my light amongst the dark. To James Van Zeeland, my friend of 25 years, thank you for reading my book on more than one occasion and for your help with the cover ideas. Your input is invaluable.

Nicci Wright

Holding Strong

Austin Macauley Publishers™
London • Cambridge • New York • Sharjah

This is a work of fiction. Names, characters, businesses, places, events, locales, and incidents are either the products of the author's imagination or used in a fictitious manner. Any resemblance to actual persons, living or dead, or actual events is purely coincidental.

A CIP catalogue record for this title is available from the British Library.

ISBN 9781398439016 (Paperback)
ISBN 9781398439023 (ePub e-book)

www.austinmacauley.com

First Published 2022
Austin Macauley Publishers Ltd®
1 Canada Square
Canary Wharf
London
E14 5AA

Chapter 1
Abbigail

OK, so my name's Abbigail. But my friends call me Abby. I'm sixteen and so sick of this house, these little boys and being broke. I live with my boyfriend Tyler and his friends though more like acquaintances. OMG, they can argue! Drives me insane! They argue over the stupidest crap. This time it's a tub of yoghurt. No wonder I don't say anything about my shit going missing. Think about it, if I was still on the street. I wouldn't have a fridge and my shit would go missing all the time. If not me; so, I'm not complaining.

So about me, I'm Abby (I told you that already). I have black hair, sixteen-year-old, a few piercings and a back tattoo to cover the scars. I live off the homeless allowance from the dole office and pay more than my fair share in bills and bloody food for the boys.

OK, so they are older than me. Brian is eighteen, Tyler, my boyfriend is twenty and the other dude that lives here is Draino, he's nineteen I think. And don't ask me why they call him Draino. I'm scared to find out.

Tyler's probably the best one out of the three of them but maybe I'm biased. Who knows anyway, it's my story so as I was saying Tyler's probably the better of the three of them.

He helped me out of a pickle when I was living on the street, hmmm can I even say that? OK I spent two nights on the street when some asshole decided he could do what he wanted with me 'cause no one else cared. So, Tyler saved me, and I've been here since. He's got a bit of ink, bit of a bad boy look you know, shaved head, big gold chain. Think half the time he just likes the company. Taking in strays off the streets. I was in a foster home after the government took me off my parent's. They said it'd be better. It wasn't. Just meant I got bullied around by a bunch of strangers instead of my own family. Kind of scary at times you know, to go through when you're young. I live in Brisbane. I mean we, live in Brisbane. Not a bad place but no country hospitality here in the city. Better opportunities though they say. I'm hoping to get a job, then maybe when I'm old enough to rent by myself; that's what I want to do. Maybe have a little flat with a veranda where I can paint or something, you know, and listen to music; yeah that'd be cool. Can't wait to get rid of this bull shit I have to put up with.

"Tyler! Ty! Let's go somewhere." I yell out to him, tired of yelling, though the only way to get heard around here. Time to break their banging little party up. "I want to go look for a job."

"What for? You get the dole with a bit extra 'cause of your age, why you got to go get a job? Hmmm."

"I just want to; the extra money would be awesome and maybe I could make some friends."

"What do you want to make friends for? You got us," he says, laughing out loud. "Just chill, we can go out later and grab something to eat yeah."

"Yeah right," I say walking away, so over this shit. *Wish I could just do me better…*I snort out loud. *What does that even mean wish I could do me better. Pfft.*

Ridiculous! I was born into shit and no doubt will die in this shit; domestic violence, child abuse. It's all the same unnecessary bull shit. This is why I do not want kids. I mean if it isn't good why bring innocent kids into it too. Isn't it bad enough so many people are stuck in these situations already? If I could live my dream life, I mean yeah cool. I get bringing family into dreams but to a living hell? Hell no. Not me and fuck that.

I got to work out how to do this. If only I could go to my appointments alone, but Tyler always comes with tells them I've been looking for work and that I don't need to do any courses I will get a job in no time. He lies to the employment agency all the time. Sucks big time but they believe what he tells them. It's like I've lost my voice and they are quite happy for him to talk for me.

"I got to go to the employment agency." I say to him. "Got to get some stuff printed out." Hopefully, he won't come with me then.

Who am I kidding? To be honest, with him, at first it made me feel safe you know. To be wrapped up in his protection but it's starting to feel stuffy. Like it's the middle of summer—no air con, no fans and no windows open. "I want to break free," good song by Queen. I remember hearing it once at the pool parlour in town, think it was on the radio or something. But that is me—I want to break free, it's scary though, you know, going from an abusive home to abusive foster care to the cramping of styles here and the bad two nights on the street. Makes me nervous…I mean what's next?

So, we end up going to the servo downtown grabbing a burger at Hungry Jacks. The manager served us; I can see the *now hiring* sign behind the counter.

I'm thinking it's now or never. Golden opportunity to apply for the job I want. So here goes.

"Hi, I was wondering if I could apply for the position going?"

Tyler starts getting agitated.

"What the hell do you think you're doing?" he asks.

"Applying for a job, I think it's the perfect opportunity."

The manager hands me an application form, watching Tyler all the while. I'm a bit nervous but I have to hold strong. I can't let Tyler ruin this for me. I borrow a pen from the manager and sit down to fill out the application form. Tyler's looking like he'd like to strangle me about now. Geez! He makes life hard.

I look at the form—previous experience, hmmm. Personal details right to work in Australia, well I'm going to need proof, hmmm I wonder if I can get my birth certificate? How do you even go about getting that? I wonder if I could ask my employment officer. Maybe she could help me? I fill out all the details as best I can and hand it back to the manager. He smiles, says thanks and we'll be in touch.

Tyler is going to be furious with me, but I don't care. I need to do this for me, you know, for my sanity. I can't deal with these boys day in day out. I need to do *me-things* sometimes. It's just hard, you know, with Tyler being so protective.

Work could be like an escape in more ways than one. I make extra money and I get time away from the house.

It wouldn't be bad working at Hungry Jacks, lots of kids my age work there. Wonder if we have anything in common though. I found it hard at school, you know, always felt like the odd one out; wrong clothes, wrong haircut. Sucks being a foster kid. By the time I paid my board out of my homeless allowance schoolbooks, shoes, uniforms, the lot. Didn't leave much to look good.

Yeah, I reckon it'll be awesome working here. Hope I get the job. Cross my fingers.

When we leave, Tyler starts on me straight away. Geez! I wish he could wait till we get home.

"So, what the fuck do you call that back there?" Tyler says.

"Don't know why you're so upset, Tyler. It'll be good for me, making extra money, having time away from home."

"Fuck off! It'll be a pain in the ass. How you gonna get there every day and who the fuck's gonna clean the house, hmmm? Did you think of that for fuck's sakes?"

"Tyler, I can walk to work by myself and I'll clean the house still." Sheesh he doesn't make this easy, does he!

"What, you trying to get rid of me, hmmm? You think you can just do what the fuck you want."

"It'll be fine Ty, no I'm not trying to get rid of you babe, just need more to do. There's things we need for the house and stuff, the extra money be good, don't you think?"

This is going to take some time to convince him that this is a good idea. I know it'll be awesome but how am I going to make him see that? So many things to think about. Think I'll go home and cook him a nice meal, clean the house up a bit and try softening his mood on me working.

We get home and I start cleaning up, but Tyler grabs my arm and swings me around. What the hell! Slap straight across my face. Oomph, fuck!

"What the hell!"

Another one.

"Tyler, no!"

I go to walk away; tears are burning in my eyes. This is not normal, right? Right? Oh my god, what have I done? I just want to run away. Then he looks me in the eyes and says, "There's more where that came from. Why defy me when I told you earlier today you don't need to work yet still! You go and apply for a job."

"I'm sorry Tyler. I just thought it'd make things better for us you know."

"No, I don't know," he says.

I look around for help to get out of this situation but Draino and Brian are just sitting there like this is an everyday occurrence. Why, why me, why now?

Unsure of what to do, I tell Tyler I'm sorry again and start cleaning up the house. My face is stinging, my eyes are burning with tears, but I can't let them fall. Not now, not ever. I will hold strong and show no weakness.

Reminds me of being home again and the memories flood back like it all happened yesterday. If I can just get through today, through this misunderstanding. It'll be fine, I'll be fine.

A few hours go by and the house is spotless. Then I start cooking dinner. Steak and vegetables tonight, might even make a mushroom sauce for the steak. It's probably gonna be a pretty shit sauce. Cooking is not really my thing you know. I never learnt to cook at home. My dad used to always say he works too hard to come home to do experimental cooking shit.

I tried once to cook but he threw the plate across the kitchen and said that if he comes home to shit like this again, we'd all be dead.

Anyway, bit off track in my thoughts, but yeah, I'm not confident in the kitchen.

"Tyler, Draino, Brian, dinners ready!"

Boys come in grunting and sitting down ready to eat. It's a quiet meal, nobody's talking. The boy's eyes are all glued to the television. Thank god. It's been a full-on day for me, I can't wait to go lay down. Whether I fall asleep quickly or not is another story. I've decided though that I will pretend I'm asleep if Tyler comes in. I can't deal with him anymore today.

Dinner's eaten now; I say goodnight to all the boys. I'm done for the day even if it is only about 7:30 pm. Tomorrow is another day.

Chapter 2
Abbigail

I wake up, not surprisingly early, it's about 6:30 am and the house is quiet; it's heaven. This is what I like about being an early riser when the boys are not. I get a few hours of serenity to wake up at my own pace. Coffee and then a shower seems the plan for now. White, no sugar, two teaspoons of coffee mmm yum; it hits the spot. I have a shower and wash my hair. I love the smell of the apple shampoo, it's only a cheap one but I've yet to find a smell I like better. I'm not really into fancy stuff. I prefer to save as much money as possible.

My face doesn't seem to have bruised, which is a good thing. I still can't believe he slapped me across the face, not once, but twice. Like where did this sudden change come from, in him? He's never hit me before, maybe it was a one-off. I did notice though he didn't show any remorse, no sign of a sorry. I wonder if that means he's going to do it again. Not sure what to do with that thought, it feels scary. I'm not so certain Tyler does care about me anymore and whether he is protective at all.

It all feels so wrong but I'm running out of options on places to go. I don't know anyone, and Tyler doesn't want me to make friends. I still don't really feel like the government did me a favour. I'm supposed to be a ward of the state till I'm legally an adult, yet here I am. I have never felt as alone as I do in this very moment, like I'm stuck in limbo. Nowhere to go but ready to move on. If only the dole office gave me enough to rent a nice little one-bedroom unit, you know. Kind of reminds me of when the police came up to the school and told me I could never go home. Emptiness; no sense of belonging to anyone or anywhere. Wondering what the future holds and who will be in it. Mum used to say to me to stay strong and hold on. She reckons all the time it'll get better. Well, mum, wherever you are I'm holding strong; I just wonder what will happen the day I cannot be strong anymore.

I wish I could've finished school but not having a home made it impossible to stay in school. I'm really hoping the job at Hungry Jacks happens so I can get somewhere. Maybe I could even look at finishing school at night or work nights and go to school during the day. Wonder how Tyler would feel about that? I don't want to be another statistic. I really want to break the mould of foster kids and be someone. Not someone big or important like a famous person or anything, just have a comfortable, crime-free, quiet life. At this point in time, I just feel like a statistic, I wonder if that feeling will ever leave me.

Trying to remember some of the good times to improve my mood a bit but it's hard to. I don't feel comfortable in the negativity I'm wearing today; it's not sitting right.

I go into the room to work out what to wear, been putting it off because I don't really want to look at Tyler at the moment. It's a beautiful sunny day outside. Gets hot here in Brisbane in summer but we're not quite there yet. It's October so we are smack bang in the middle of spring. Might wear a flowery sundress that goes to my knees with shoestring straps. I like the shades of pink and red in it.

Oh crap, I just realised it's Tyler's dole day. The boys will be drinking tonight. They'll wake up soon too knowing they have money in the bank. Brian and Draino get paid the same day.

Better get organised instead of sitting here dwelling on crap I can't change. I start the dishes; Tyler comes up behind me and wraps his arms around my waist, kissing me on the neck. I am not sure whether to freeze up or melt.

Things are going to have to change and I'm not sure how Ty is going to feel about it, or how he is going to react. I'm nervous.

"I love you." He whispers in my ear and for the first time I'm not sure how to reply. But I say it back. It's what he expects, and I want to keep the peace.

"I really like you in that dress, why don't you come back to bed for a while," he says. I'm feeling nervous now what do I say to that because the last thing I feel like doing is going back to bed with Ty.

"Maybe later," I say.

"OK, I will hold you to it," he says calmly, giving me another kiss on the jawline, before I hand him his coffee that I just made.

We sit down in silence for a while and then Tyler starts the list of things to do today.

"So later we'll go down to the smoke shop to grab some smokes, head over to the Aldi and grab some food. I'll send the other two home with that and you and me can go get some grog yeah?"

"Sounds like a plan," I reply.

"OK cool, so you'll be with me all day, babe."

He leans in for a kiss and a cuddle, I feel nervous for the first time in showing him affection.

I've never felt so uncertain, well I probably have just not for a while you know. It really rattled me when he slapped me yesterday. I'm not sure if there's more to come or not and I'm a little scared. Don't get me wrong I've experienced worse, but it doesn't mean I'm going to enjoy it or go looking for it because I'm not that type of person.

"What time is it, babe?"

I look down at my phone and reply, "Nine, babe."

"OK well I'll go have a shower and we can get this show on the road, yeah."

"Yeah, no worries," I reply.

After a few minutes and another ciggie he gets up and goes and has a shower. I finish off my coffee and get organised to go brush my teeth.

It's about 20 minutes later and we're standing at the door with the Aldi bags ready to go shopping. First stop is the tobacconist.

So, we head off toward Toombul Shopping Centre. Our crib's a little house across from the units on London Street at Nundah. We walk pretty much everywhere we need to go and it's only a 15-minute walk to the Toombul shops. Just walking straight down Sandgate Road.

I'd love a little unit there at London Street I think, they're only one-bedroom units. It'd be awesome. They were done up a few years back and now they look really awesome. They *rendered* the outside I think, that's what they call it. and they put some nice timber trimmings. They're awesome anyway.

"Abby! For crying out loud, I've called you a dozen times where are you at girl?"

"Shit, sorry, was just day-dreaming," I reply. Wonder how many times he's called me? Oops.

"So," he continues, "As I was saying we have finished here, now we're off to Aldi."

"Yeah, no worries," I say and pull the token for the trolley out of my purse.

So, we've done the shopping and the boys are taking it home. Time to toddle off to the bottle shop.

Tyler gets a carton of beer and a couple of bottles of that $10 vodka; shit it's gonna be a big night.

Sitting down while listening to music, my phone starts ringing. It's about 3:30 pm and the boys are drunk as anything. I walk away from the rowdiness to answer my phone. I don't recognise the number.

"Hello," I say as I answer the phone.

"Hi, this is Adam the manager at Hungry Jacks, I received an application form from you the other day?"

"Oh, hi Adam. Thanks yes, this is Abbigail."

"Hi Abbigail, yes I was wondering if you would be able to come in for an interview tomorrow at 2 pm?"

"Yes, that would be fantastic, thanks."

"Great see you then."

"Thank you, Adam. Yes, I'll see you then."

I hang up the phone and go to head back to the boys not sure how I'm going to tell Tyler, I turn around and he is right there behind me.

"Who the fuck is Adam?" he yells at me.

Oh, shit, this isn't going to go well. He's already got his back up and he is drunk. I look at his face and I freeze. The blackest eyes are looking at me and I'm beginning to wonder not if I'll be beaten, that is a given; but whether I will survive to tell the tale.

The look on his face takes me back to the times my dad beat me up and I know there is no escaping the wrath of his fury.

Chin up, I face him. "Adam is the manager at Hungry Jacks. I have an interview tomorrow."

"Like fuck you do!" he states. And I know I'm not backing down; I feel like a fool but either way, I need to face this.

"I am going to the interview Tyler and if I don't get the job it'll be fine. How about I go cook us up a feed, we got heaps of awesome food today."

Smack! "Oh fuck, Tyler no! Please don't do this," I scream and it's on, he just keeps thumping into my head with a closed fist. No slapping this time. I scream again, but no one comes to help. He grabs a handful of my hair and throws me to the ground. I cop a kick in the gut which doubles me up then one to the head; all goes black.

Chapter 3
Draino

"What the fuck?" I say to Brian. Abby walked off a minute ago, I think her phone rang. Tyler followed her which made me nervous. He slapped her a couple of times yesterday and I really wanted to say something. I guess I can admit it to you I've had a crush something bad on Abby for a while now, but she's with Ty. I don't like it but at the moment I'm living under his roof and so is she. I can't do nothing to get us out of this situation, so I did nothing. Don't get me wrong I feel like a piece of shit for just sitting there but nothing else I can do.

Anyway, I heard Abby scream; so, I get up to see what's going on. I know Tyler followed her and it doesn't sound good.

As I get around the corner, I see Abby doubled up on the ground and Tyler kicks her in the face. She must have passed out because she's not making any noise.

I dial 000 on my phone and say ambulance and police. I'll be fucked if he's getting away with it this time. Omg, what do I do? I just want to hold her and protect her, how dare he? They're on their way so I barge past Tyler to Abby to feel for a pulse.

"What the fuck Tyler! What have you done to her!"

"Fuck-off," he says to me. "She asked for it, fucking interview tomorrow at Hungry Jacks with Adam; let's see her make it now."

He goes to kick her again and I push him over.

"Fucking leave her alone," I scream at him. I'm spitting as I talk, I am so fucking angry at him.

I hear the sirens; he looks at me.

"You called the fucking cops, you fucking dog."

"She needs medical attention." And that's all I say to him as I kneel down next to her. Her face is a mess looks like a broken nose, two black eyes, fuck her face is a mess; poor beautiful Abby. I vow never to see her like this again. I'm going to protect her.

Police come in first to secure the scene for the ambos, Tyler puts up a bit of a fight; that's good. It'll keep him locked up a bit longer. That's what I need while he's locked up, I'll get all mine and Abby's stuff out of this hell hole.

The ambulance officers come in and Abby is still out cold. I'm freaking out. "Can I go with Abby to the hospital in the ambulance?"

"Yes, that's fine."

I'm shaking so bad; god, I hope she pulls through.

They load her into the ambulance, I climb in onto the seat. I hold her hand and make a heap of promises, I hope she lets me keep them. I'm not a religious person but for the first time in my life, I say a prayer in my head. Well not sure how to pray, but I hope God heard me.

I'm not sure what to feel either, but damn it hurts to think I let this happen.

They take Abby straight through for a CT scan to see what's happening in the brain. She still hasn't woken up.

The doctor comes in and asks me a few questions. I tell them as much as I know, and explain I saw Tyler kick her in the face and that is all I saw.

I called the police and ambulance. She's been out for a good half an hour already; I'm worried she won't wake up and I voice this to the doctor.

"She will wake up, it's just a matter of time. The CT scan showed normal brain activity; but she took a hard kick to the head, all you can do is be here when she wakes up."

I nod; totally out of words.

"Does she have any family; anyone we need to notify of her whereabouts?"

"No, she was a foster kid but got kicked out about six months ago. We've all been living together since. I don't think she'll have anywhere to live now, and I need to find somewhere too."

The doctor looks at me and nods seriously. It's like I can see his brain ticking over but not sure what he is thinking.

"I'll make some phone calls." He says and walks away.

OK. I wish I could see what he was thinking. I'm sure it's important.

But for obvious reasons, I can't see what he's thinking. Abby is still asleep. I'm going to contact Adam at Hungry Jacks and see if I can reschedule her interview for her. It's a damn shame he cracked it; I just hope her opportunity for independence is not lost entirely. I'm not going anywhere till she wakes up though. I really hope she wakes up soon.

I'm sitting there in a trance, stressed to the max thinking of all the things I need to do. Not just to get me somewhere, but Abby too. I can't believe I let it go this far. I should have knocked him out when he slapped her yesterday.

Next thing I hear is Abby groan. I stand up quickly and rush to her side which makes her flinch.

I cringe.

"Abby, you're safe now," I say, "You're in the hospital, I'm so sorry but Tyler beat you pretty bad."

"I feel like shit," She mumbles, her face is all swollen and she's finding it hard to talk.

"I'll go find a nurse," I say to her and walk away reluctantly. I just want to wrap her in cotton wool and keep her safe from the world.

"Abby's awake now, can you please go help her?"

"I'll just get the Doctor and I'll be right there," she says.

"Thank you," I reply.

I go back to Abby's room and tell her that the nurse and doctor are coming. She's shaking and I'm shit scared. I'm not sure what to do. Maybe it's shock but maybe it's more serious.

"Can I hold your hand?" I say and she reaches her hand out. When her hand is secure in mine, I tell her it'll be OK. I tell her Tyler is locked up at the moment and she is safe. That does it; she breaks down crying; big wracking sobs. I feel the tears slide down my cheeks too. It's breaking me that she is so broken. There's not a damn thing I can do to make it better either.

"Why?" she cries.

"I don't know but I do know I am so sorry; I should have stopped him sooner. I saw you walk away and then I heard you scream. You were out cold before I even got around the corner; so, I called the cops and an ambulance."

"You called the cops on Ty?" she asks.

I just nod. What can I say?

"He's gonna kick you out after he kicks your ass. Draino what were you thinking what are you going to do? What the fuck am I going to do?"

And the wracking sobs are back I hold her hand still there's nothing I can say; I have no answers yet.

The doctor and nurse walk in. I say to Abby that I gotta go back to the house and grab some stuff; will she be OK for an hour or so? She says she'll be fine but I have my doubts. The doctor reassures me she will not be discharged, and I feel that I can leave for an hour or so.

I squeeze her hand in a gentle reassuring way and walk out, each step is killing me; I have to get our stuff before Tyler gets out of the watch house.

First stop though is Hungry Jacks, to talk to the manager about rescheduling her interview.

Half an hour later I walk into Hungry Jacks. It's about 6:30 pm already but I can see the manager's name tag, ADAM. Excellent.

"Hi Adam, you don't know me but I'm a friend of Abbigail's. She has a job interview tomorrow, I believe?"

"Hi, yes, she does, how can I help you?" he says.

"Umm yeah, there's been a bit of an incident and she's in hospital at the moment. I was wondering if I can reschedule her interview for her because she currently can't, but I know she really wants the job here."

I'm fully nervous and shaking but he replies pretty quickly.

"Oh my god," he says. "What happened? Is she going to be OK?"

"Oh, she will be OK, she just woke up. I'm not sure how long it will take her to recover but I'm guessing she will be

OK to work in a couple of weeks?" I say while crossing my fingers, hoping that he will be okay with that.

"Tell her to take as long as she needs. This is my card, ask her to call me and reschedule as soon as she is up for it."

I shake his hand and walk out. I really have to get to the house and get all our stuff out before Tyler gets back. He is going to flip out of control, I need to be long gone and keep Abby safe by then.

So, I head off to our crib, quickly speed walking but it's almost a jog. I walk into Tyler and Abby's room and it breaks my heart to remember all the times I heard him fucking her and I was in the next room; wishing it was me. I grab a couple of shopping bags and find her draws, chucking as much stuff in as I can. Couple more bags and my stuff. One more bag each in the bathroom, few tins of food, couple of packets of shit out of the pantry, I turn around and Brian is watching me.

"What are you doing?" he says to me.

"Abby woke up not long ago. She's a mess Brian and we just sat back and let it happen."

"Not much we could've done," he replies.

"That's weak shit bro and you know it."

"Your right," he says. "But who are we to interfere."

"Her friends too," I reply with a scowl on my face.

"You love her, don't you?" He says to me. I look at him, give a curt nod and stand up ready to walk out.

"Look after her. I'll stay here and try to talk Ty down." He says to me. I shake his hand and leave. One last look back and I'm glad she's not here to see the sorrow of the unknown in my eyes.

Chapter 4
Abbigail

I'm scared shitless. The doctor told me my nose is broken, I have two black eyes I can barely see out of and my mouth is so swollen it's hard to talk; I keep drooling because it's too hard to swallow. Wonder why Draino came with me? At first it scared me. I thought Tyler had sent him to keep an eye on me but call it gut instinct, I don't think that's the reason. He looked scared too. I started bleeding and the doctor thinks that I may have been pregnant. When Tyler kicked me in the gut; he killed his own child. I feel weird but grateful. There is nothing to tie me to him in the future. I didn't want kids anyway. I'm still a kid myself; shit.

I recall a phone call vaguely but not sure why. My head feels so hazy and I feel so sick and sore. My face is too sore but itchy from the morphine they gave me for the pain. Couldn't scratch my nose if I wanted to.

I kind of feel like I felt when I got hit by the car as a kid. Always hoped I'd never feel like this again but here we are. I gotta work out how to get my stuff from the house. Once Tyler is out of the watch-house, I don't have a hope in hell of getting my stuff back. The doctor already told me they won't be releasing me today though. I can't go back to him, it's not an option. Where am I going to live? That triggers my memory of the phone call. Damn, I got a job interview tomorrow! There is no way they are going to give me the job if I turn up looking like this! He ruined my opportunity. He would be quite proud of that fact too; the asshole.

I don't expect Draino to come back though.

Just as I think that, he walks through the door loaded up with bags. I look at him.

"I got as much of your stuff as I could carry," he says.

"Thanks," I say dubiously. "What are you doing here Draino? I'm not going back to Tyler."

"Thank god for that," he says. "This is my stuff too. I called the cops on Tyler, we're both out on our asses," he says with a cocky grin.

"Oh, shit Draino, what were you thinking?"

He sits down next to me, the cocky grin gone and he looks nervous as all hell.

"Abbigail, I've never said anything before because you were with Ty, but I really do like you. When he slapped you the other day? It broke my fucking heart to sit there and do nothing. I couldn't do it again, besides, you were out cold before I got around the corner."

"Draino, what…?"

"Just listen," he says to me in a quiet voice, "Hear me out."

So, I sit back and wait for him to finish.

"I couldn't give you a home, still can't." His head hangs down like he's ashamed. "But I went to Hungry Jacks and Adam, the manager, said to give him a call when you get out of the hospital and are ready to work." He hands me Adam's business card.

"I gotta find a home and a job myself but I'm hoping we can stay in touch anyway and maybe, in time, we can be more." He looks so scared but continues, "I know you don't like men much at the moment and I don't blame you. None have done right by you so far and I don't expect you to think I'd be any different."

"Draino don't—" I start to say. But he shakes his head.

"I want you to find your feet Abbigail, and in the meantime, I'll find mine too. We are still young, and we got our whole lives ahead of us. Let's not rush into decisions either way, yeah?"

"What is your real name?" I say to him.

He laughs and says, "John Paul Smith."

"Lol," I say.

"How the hell did you end up Draino?"

"I got dared to drink the biggest beer bong ever at a party once," he says. "I drained it good 'n' proper before I passed out. I've been called Draino instead of Johnny ever since."

"Mind if I call you Johnny?" I say.

"Not at all princess," he says.

And I'm dozing off to sleep again.

Chapter 5
Draino

Abbigail has fallen back asleep and I am totally exhausted. I curl up in the seat in her room deciding to stay with her because I don't feel like she's safe if I leave. It's not like I got anywhere to go anyway.

A nurse comes in about 9:00 pm and asks if I'm staying with her. I agree that I won't be leaving her alone anytime soon.

She informs me that the police rang to warn them that Tyler has been released, however, there's an emergency domestic violence order in place. They are to call the police if Tyler turns up. They faxed his mug shot through anyway, but I tell the nurse I know who to watch for.

If I can just catch a few zzz's before Tyler turns up, I'll be better able to deal with him I reckon.

I close my eyes and drift off.

Feels like only a few minutes later I hear Tyler shouting at the nurses. Unsure of what to do, I stay in the room hoping cops are on the way. I don't want to walk out, then he'd know what room she's in.

I look over and notice Abby has heard him too. I put my finger to my mouth to signal for her to be quiet and I walk over to hold her hand. She's crying, it breaks me. Silent tears fall down her face and she or I can't even wipe them away; the bruising is so bad. I don't want to hurt her by trying.

Security is out on the ward now, I can hear them; cops must be on their way. I stroke her thumb hoping to bring her some comfort but not sure it's working.

No one has come in yet, so Tyler doesn't know where she is.

I feel like I'm holding my breath waiting for his tirade to end. And then I hear the handcuffs click and Tyler scream out to Abby.

"You're dead bitch! Putting me through this shit. You'll keep!"

She whimpers and I shhhh out loud; I don't know what to do.

I feel so hopeless.

A good twenty minutes later a nurse comes in to check on Abby and I ask her for a word in the hallway.

After she checks Abby over, blood pressure, temperature, pain levels, etc. I follow her into the hallway.

"Is there a social worker or someone I can talk to about finding somewhere for Abbigail to live?" I ask. She looks at me with the saddest look on her face and replies.

"The social worker from the hospital will come and see her tomorrow, they will find a home for her."

"She won't go back to foster care or share accommodation," I tell her.

"She won't have to," she replies.

I calm down a bit with that information on hand and go back to check on Abbigail.

I walk into the room and she looks at me, it kills me to see her face so messed up and her eyes look so scared.

"Is he gone? I don't think I can deal with him again." She cries.

"Shhh, he's gone. Take a deep breath," I tell her calmly.

It's going to take a while for her to realise she doesn't have to do this alone. I know they'll find her somewhere safe to live and help her get set up in this job. She's so young and has gone through so much already. I went through a lot too but she's such a sweet girl; she never deserved any of this that life gave her.

I settle back in the chair, so she knows I'm not leaving her; not just yet. I know I have to give her space to grow and be her, the best of her she can be. I really want to support her, but I think more than anything she needs to learn the best person to rely on is herself. I learnt that and it took a while but I've been better for it. I got a bit relaxed at Tyler's, but I was there to keep an eye on her. I've known Ty for a while now, he found me on the streets too. Took me in when I was seventeen. I've seen how he treated women before Abby and she is beautiful inside and out. I have just never seen him lose it so bad before, but I've never known him to be with anyone as long as Abby either. So, I guess time changes everything and everyone.

Need to try to get some sleep. They won't let Tyler out tonight again; he'll be in, till court tomorrow.

Chapter 6
Abbigail

I wake up and Johnny is asleep on the chair still. I stare at him through the slits that are my eyes at the moment and wonder why I have never seen him like this before.

Who is this Johnny? Draino is no more. I heard him talking to the nurse in the hallway last night and I wonder if not a foster home and if not share accommodation where will I end up. I ache all over so bad. I want to ring for the nurse for some painkillers, but I don't want Johnny to be disturbed by the noise. So, I just lay there, watching him.

I must have dozed off watching Johnny sleep because when I wake up the nurse is doing my observations and Johnny is talking to her; asking how I am doing.

"Morning," I mumble to the room.

"Morning," says Johnny with a smile.

"Morning," says the nurse. "How are you feeling? Are you in any pain?"

"Yeah, the pain's pretty bad at the moment," I say.

"OK, we will give you something for that," she replies. "Is there anything else I can get you?"

"An orange juice or a coffee?"

"I will grab you one of each," she replies and I feel relieved. I like my morning coffee, but some juice would be heaven.

"Did you get much sleep?" I ask Johnny.

"I got enough," he replies. "How about you?"

"I got enough."

The nurse comes back with pain relief meds and juice and coffee. "Feels like a resort." I snort-laugh even though it hurts to do so.

Johnny laughs too, he can see the funny side of us mere mortals, been waited on. Or maybe he just thought my laugh was funny; I snort-laugh again. Think the morphine has kicked in.

Chapter 7

Draino

Think the morphine kicked in since Abby laughed one minute, which I cannot deny is the cutest laugh ever, then she fell straight to sleep.

I really need to leave her for a while, but I'm worried how she'll feel if I'm not here when she wakes up.

"Can I leave my stuff here for a while with Abbigail?" I ask the nurse.

"Of course," she replies.

I ask her for a piece of paper and write Abbigail a note, letting her know I'll be back.

My first stop is the courthouse. I want some answers for Abbigail. I go in and look on the board for Tyler's name. There it is Tyler Stuart courtroom 8. I walk in and take a seat. He should be up soon because he's in custody.

I don't have to wait long; the public prosecutor starts her spiel on charges. Hell, assault of an officer, breach of a domestic violence order, public nuisance, intoxicated in a public place, and the list went on. Six months imprisonment. Good, that gives Abbigail a chance to get settled and him a chance to get over her and stay away. Next stop is the building site down the road I want to get a job, even being a labourer would be awesome. I reach my destination and go straight to the site office. I knock on the portable office door and stand back to wait. I don't have to wait long before a bloke walks out.

"Can I help you?" he says.

"Hi, I was wondering if you have any labourer jobs going at the moment?"

"Yeah, a couple, you got any experience?"

"No can't say I do, but I'm keen to work and have full availability."

"OK no worries, report here tomorrow morning at 6:00 am sharp, ask for Will, he will show you the ropes. You have to do what he asks you to, OK."

"No worries, thank you, I'll be here."

Now I need to get back to the hospital and check on Abbigail.

Not sure if she's awake yet, but I can't wait to tell her the good news.

It takes me about forty minutes to get back to the Royal Brisbane Hospital where Abbigail is.

I walk in and she's ringing her hands together agitated.

"Hi," I say. "How are you feeling."

"Oh hey, I was worried you'd left; I got your note though, thank you."

"Sorry princess, I had to go take care of some things, I have some good news though."

"Oh really, why what happened?"

"Well, Tyler got six months in prison. So, he won't be annoying you for a while, and I got a job; I start tomorrow morning at 6 am."

"Wow, OK," she says. "That's a lot to take in. Six months in prison for hitting me?"

"Not just hitting you, he assaulted a police officer and they charged him for coming up here last night as well."

"Oh OK," she says.

"Yeah, so I'll be working on a building site as a labourer," I tell her.

"That's really great, wow congratulations," says Abbigail.

You can see she's trying to smile, but it is strained. Also, her face is so swollen you can barely see it move. She's got a lot on her mind at the moment.

We keep chatting till the nurse comes in and gives Abby another dose of pain medication.

It's hard to watch her, the bruising has really come out now and she looks at me through the slits that once were eye lids. I really hope he gets a hard time in prison being a woman basher; he probably will.

Abbigail looks at me and I melt. She's so precious.

"Has the social worker been here to see you yet?" I ask.

"Not yet."

"OK, I wonder what time they will come around."

"Not sure," she replies. "But I could use a nap, are you going out again?"

"Nope. I'll be here when you wake up," I say. "Get some rest."

She dozes off again and I'm glad she's resting up. I'm wondering when they will send the social worker around so that I know Abbigail has somewhere to go, before I find somewhere to go. I know Tyler won't be back at the crib for a few months but still, it doesn't feel right to go back there with Abbigail. She doesn't need to see the place again, not after what she went through there.

I realise, though, it gives me the perfect opportunity to go grab the rest of our stuff and I can have a word with Brian. Let him know that Tyler won't be back for a while. The only problem is the only place we have to stash all our stuff at the moment is the hospital room. When the nurse comes back in, I might ask her to locate the social worker and see how long till they can see Abby. She really needs somewhere to go when she gets released. It doesn't seem like they are in a hurry to get her out of here though. I wonder what time the doctor does their rounds.

Chapter 8
Abbigail

I wake up again for what feels like the tenth time today. I'm so tired, but maybe it's just my body's way of saying stop, so I can heal. Johnny is curled up on the seat asleep again as well. It's been a full-on couple of days, and I'm scared as hell about what the future holds. The social worker hasn't been around yet and I'm not sure if I'll have a home to go to when I get released from here. I'm still not sure why I'm still in here especially just for a broken nose. Maybe it was because I was out for a while.

It's a couple of hours later when a lady walks in.

"Hi, you must be Abbigail, my name is Alecia. I am the social worker here at the hospital," she states.

At that, Johnny sits up straight still half asleep.

"Hi, yes I am Abbigail," I say.

"And I'm Johnny," he says as he stands up to shake her hand.

"I hear you have recently become homeless," says Alecia.

"Yeah had a bit of bad luck," I say, trying to smile with tears in my eyes. Johnny gets up and comes over to me holding my hand. He is a great emotional support at the moment; just what I need.

Alecia continues, "I have spoken to a lady by the name of Sandra at the Domestic Violence Action Centre, they have a one-bedroom unit become available recently and have stated that it is yours, if you are interested?"

"Oh my god! Are you serious?" I say, my mind has been totally blown away.

Johnny gives a massive smile but asks the logical question, "Where about is it located? How much a fortnight?"

"Glad you asked," says Alecia. "It is located at Toombul so it's not too far from where you used to live. It costs 150 a week so that is $300 a fortnight. Do you think you could manage that Abbigail?"

"Sounds perfect," I say as I burst into tears. I can't believe my luck. I have my dream home and it doesn't even matter what it looks like inside or out.

Alecia goes on to tell us that it is a block of units specifically for domestic violence victims and I can have a two-year lease. The block is under constant video surveillance and they have a security company that checks on the units regularly. It sounds like exactly what I need at the moment until I build my confidence up again. It also gives me a buffer for when Tyler gets out of prison in six months; with that, I'm relying on the fact he won't get parole. At least I hope he won't, or he could be out next month.

Johnny looks relieved too.

"Are there any high schools near Toombul?" I ask.

"Yes," she replies. "Aviation High is at Toombul, not far from the units. Are you considering going back to school, Abbigail?"

"Yeah, I was actually. I think I would like to finish high school at least. I kind of figure I could work part-time while I go through school too."

"Sounds like a perfect idea," say both Johnny and Alecia at the same time.

"So, do you know when I can be released?" I say to Alecia.

"You will be able to stay in here for a couple of days until the unit is ready. It is fully furnished, so all you will need are your personal belongings."

"Oh OK," I say. I still can't believe they are keeping me in hospital for so long.

Johnny turns around and looks at me. "I gotta go find somewhere to live soon princess, but I'll come back here when I'm done if that's OK?" he asks.

"Can you find somewhere for Johnny to live too?" Abbigail asks Alecia.

"I wish I could," she states. "Unfortunately, because he is not a patient my hands are tied." I'm disappointed in the system for that, but I expected as much. Johnny is OK with it though, so I guess that's OK.

He leaves shortly after to go find somewhere to live. I have no idea where he is going to end up, it's stressful.

I want to make sure he's fine, just like he did for me, but I'm stuck in this hospital bed.

He's a grown boy, though, he will sort something out. Geez, he's already got a job; lucky bugger. I am so overwhelmed by the support at the moment. It's crazy, you know. When I went into foster care, I felt like I was left for dead and the system doesn't get anything right. It seems I was wrong though. I don't know, maybe the system itself is screwed up, but the private sector gets funding to fix up the screw-up of a system. It seems so weird. My mind feels numb right now. I can't believe I have my own unit to live in for the next two years. I am excited, nervous, exhausted and tired, all at the same time. Even though it's hard to get too excited when you're in so much pain. I'm getting sick of being doped up on painkillers. There's nothing I can do about it at the moment anyway because I am in too much pain not to take them. I'm thinking a shower might be a good idea though; it's going to be hard to wash my face.

The doctor said I will have to have a curettage when he came around earlier. I'm not sure what it involves exactly but I'm not too thrilled about it. I never told Johnny about the baby, I'm not sure I will ever tell anybody. It was a blessing though because I can't look after myself yet. In a couple of days, it will all change. Life is going to be so much different but a *better different*. Not like when I went into foster care and it was a *worse different*.

I get out of the shower. I knocked my nose trying to clean the dried blood off my face and it's really hurting now. I hope the nurse comes soon with some pain relief again. I feel exhausted. The shower, which would normally leave me feeling better, has exhausted me. I think I'll try to get some natural sleep in before they come to a dose me up again. I wonder if the drug-induced sleep counts as sleep. Silly question. And my eyes close slowly as I drift off into a fitful sleep.

Chapter 9
Draino

I ran into an old mate while I was out looking for somewhere to live. I went to check the noticeboard at Toombul Shopping Centre to see if there were any rooms for rent. There was one but when I called the number the fella seemed really gruff. I didn't like the sound of him at all. So anyway, back to Darren, my friend that I ran into; he just got a two-bedroom unit not far from where I was living in Nundah and he's looking for someone to rent the second bedroom. So I go with him back to his crib and check it out. I reckon it's perfect so, I tell him I got a job. I start at six tomorrow morning. He's stoked for me and says I can move straight in.

I can't believe it's all coming together so easily. Perfect too. Abbigail's got a place to move into by herself in a couple of days. I can't imagine I'll be relying on the dole any longer. Not now since I got a job.

I go back up to the hospital to let Abby know the good news. I can't wait to tell her. I'm so excited. Been a long time but everything's going so well at the moment; I just hope it stays like this.

It takes me a good forty minutes and I'm back in Abby's room at the hospital.

She's sound asleep so I just sit there admiring the sleeping beauty before me. I'm going to go back to the house and grab all our stuff, take it around to my new home. When Abby gets her unit in a couple of days, I'll drop her stuff around to her after I finish work.

I'm proud of her for wanting to finish her high school education. It's a big step forward and I'm not like Tyler. I'm going to support her hundred percent in her plans for the future. Even if it means leaving me behind as much as that hurts to think; it's not about me. Hasn't been for a long time. I just want her to be safe and happy.

The social worker left a card for Abby for the Domestic Violence Action Centre. Looks like she has to call them. I wonder if she has credit on her phone. If she doesn't, I can lend her my phone anyway.

As I'm watching her sleep, I see her eyes flutter open.

"Hey princess, you're awake," I say with a smile.

"Yeah, you're back. How did you go finding somewhere to live?"

"Good." I smile. "I ran into an old mate Darren and he's just got a two-bedroom unit at Nundah, so I won't be far away."

"Oh, that's so good," she says sleepily with a smile. She looks exhausted. I'm really worried about her. I suspect something else has happened she doesn't want to talk about but I know she will tell me in time if she wants to talk about it.

"You OK?" I ask her.

"Yeah, I'm OK, just so tired and in so much pain."

"Yeah, to be expected, you know I'm here if you need to talk about anything, yeah?"

"Yeah, I know Johnny, thank you. I'm OK though just tired."

"Did you have credit to ring DVAC, or did you want to borrow my phone?"

"Nah, it's OK. The nurse bought a phone in before while you were gone."

"OK, so everything is getting sorted?"

"Yeah, they will organise some paperwork and they said I can get a bond loan to cover the bond. I just can't move in before it's approved otherwise, they won't give me the loan."

"OK, so what do you have to do to get that happening?" I ask.

"They're sending some forms through to the social worker for me to fill out. I'm not allowed to leave the hospital yet so the social worker is going to do as much as she possibly can."

"OK, so you can sit back and relax?"

"I have to get the rest of my stuff somehow from Tyler's place."

"Yeah about that," I say. "I was going to go pick it all up soon if you are fine here?"

"Yeah, I'll be fine."

"OK cool, and I'll take all our stuff to my new crib. Then when you get out I can bring yours around for you and check out the new bachelorette pad." I laugh, Abbigail follows suite.

"That sounds awesome," she says.

"So, I'll head off now. Will you be OK if I stay at my new place tonight or do you want me to come back?" I ask softly.

"I'll be OK. Tyler is in jail, yeah?"

"Yeah, he is."

"Well, I will be fine. The nurses here are really good and I feel safe. Thank you for all your help, Johnny, I really appreciate it."

"Don't sweat the small stuff," I say with a wink.

I take a last look at Abby before I leave the room. Despite all the bruising, she looks pale and washed out. She needs this time to recover from the ordeal.

It'll be a few more months before the school year starts next year so she will have time to settle in and get into a new routine.

I'm pretty certain she will get the job at Hungry Jacks too; she is going to need it.

I catch the train back to Nundah train station and go straight to Tyler's. Brian is sitting on the couch looking stressed. I'm not sure how this is going to go but we'll see how it plays out.

"Hi, Brian," I say.

"Yo! What's happening," he says.

I sit down for the long conversation filling him in on Tyler's whereabouts and how Abbigail is doing in the hospital.

I tell him that Tyler came up to the hospital last night creating a scene and got carted away by the cops again. I tell him Abby's nose is broken and that she was out of it for a good while after she arrived at the hospital.

I don't tell him I suspect Abby is hiding something about what happened, but I tell him she got a unit she can move into in a couple of days. I also told him about my getting a new crib and that I'm there to pick all our stuff up. I ask him what he's going to do for rent and stuff, but he's not sure the real estate will let him stay. The lease is in Tyler's name only.

It's a full-on conversation but Brian and I have been close for a few years and it flows easily.

Brian lets me use a suitcase he has, and we find as many Aldi bags as we can. I feel weird going back into Tyler and Abbigail's room, but it needs to be done. Even worse is going through draws and shit because I don't know what Abbigail's is or what Tyler's is.

I get there eventually, it takes a good couple of hours though. I'm so tired though. I got a crappy sleep in an armchair at the hospital and it's been a full-on day. Going to take all this stuff back to Darren's and mine and crash. I have to get up for work in the morning. Then I want to go see Abby after work.

Chapter 10

Abbigail

I briefly wake up for dinner and then fall back asleep. I'm not sure if it's because I lost the baby or not, but I feel so weak. I don't want to have to tell Johnny that I miscarried but I'm suspecting he already knows there's more to the story than I'm saying. They have me booked in for the curettage in the morning which is good. Johnny will be at work, so I don't have to explain why I'm going off for a procedure.

I don't want to jump into a relationship, but I think he understands that. I'm not sure I ever want one again, but I know time heals old wounds.

He's been so good to me these last couple of days I don't know how I'll ever repay him.

I've still got a few months to get sorted before school starts. I really hope that Aviation High will take me as a student. I'm scared, excited, nervous, anxious and god knows what else I'm feeling.

It's getting late, I should stop thinking and get some sleep, tomorrow is a new day and I have to have the procedure.

Chapter 11
Draino

I catch a cab from Tyler's to Darren's. There's more stuff than I originally thought there would be. Save me doing two trips, it's already getting late. My alarm is set for 4 am. I'm going to have to sort through my stuff in the morning. I know I have hi-vis wear and steel caps amongst my stuff. I don't have a hard hat but I'm hoping I can sort that out tomorrow.

I'll ask Will as soon as I get there.

Worse comes to worst, my employment agency might buy me one, since I got a job that needs it.

I drop all our belongings in my room where there's a bed, thank god.

"Darren, you got any spare sheets, mate, so I can make the bed?"

"Yeah, in the hall cupboard there's a bunch, help yourself."

"Great thanks, then I'm going to crash. My alarm is set for 4:00 am. Hope that's OK, I got to sort through clothes for work."

"Yeah, all good," says Darren. "Goodnight."

I go to the hall cupboard get a couple of sheets and a pillowcase. Make the bed and jump straight in it, I'll have a shower in the morning.

Lights out.

Chapter 12

Abbigail

It's a new day. I have the curettage today, scared a bit I must admit. It's already 7:30 am when I wake, and Johnny will be at work. It's kind of scary going through things like this alone when you don't know what the hell they are talking about.

It's always times like this, I wish I had a mum, but not the mum I had. If that makes sense. My mother was never very supportive. I have no doubt she didn't put up a fight for me. I never saw them again. I've seen when I was in foster care that some mothers got visitation and tried to fight the Department of child safety, for their kids. Not my family. I didn't get much stuff from the house either, she dropped it off at the foster home and I never saw her.

It took a week for them to find me a foster home, so I had to stay in a detention centre till they found one. I never worked out what I did to deserve this. I guess it's just my lot in life; that's what my foster mum said anyway.

Some kids put up with shit their whole lives and are not taken off their parents but some are and maybe, some don't end up where I am. I'm not talking about in a hospital, I mean homeless. Maybe some get a good home.

I know a lot don't though.

I've spoken to Sandra from Domestic Violence Action Centre and the social worker here has lodged the bond loan forms I filled out. I just need to sign them tomorrow and go get the keys. They're going to meet me at the unit. I'm so nervous and excited all at the same time. The social worker said I have to take my lease to the dole office too. Apparently, I can get more rent assistance now. It'll make it a bit easier, but I won't have to worry about anyone else eating my food either. Oh My God! I won't have to worry about anyone eating my food. I'm smiling at that thought, on the inside anyway, outside I ache too much to smile yet. Thank god the morphine's stopped now though, I'm just taking paracetamol and ibuprofen.

The orderly comes to wheel me down for the procedure before I have breakfast. It's been near impossible to eat, but I have been trying to.

Hopefully, in a couple more days the swelling will go down and the bruising will start to fade.

It's stopped getting worse, so I guess that's something.

I feel like I'm stuck in my head today. The thoughts are coming fast and thick and the more I try to stop them the faster they come.

Apart from the past and present, I'm thinking about the future too. I'm looking forward to working hopefully and going to school. Also, I am looking forward to this one-bedroom unit. When I was homeless for the two nights, I stayed in a condemned building I found. The windows were boarded up and the place was graffitied, anything would be better than that.

They finished the procedure and I'm back on the ward. Not as scary as I thought it would be, so that is a bonus. Still trying to work out what I want to do after I finish high school, maybe I'm getting a bit ahead of myself.

I manage to eat a piece of toast and a bowl of porridge with orange juice and coffee, I did well.

I'm wondering what time Johnny will finish work. I'm proud of him for going and getting a job. I'm also forever grateful for him being there for me too.

He's taken on a lot in the last few days, what with getting our stuff out of Tyler's and everything else. He would have had a late-night last night, getting all our stuff back to Darren's place. Then work bright and early. He said he's coming around after work and I'm grateful.

Friends will be good. I mean between school and work I'm not going to have a lot of spare time. Well, I couldn't imagine I would anyway.

I want to get into art as well, I'm really hoping it's a subject at school still.

I want to do painting at home too. I like painting people's faces. I make them up in my mind and sometimes, I even sketch them. It's relaxing.

I'm hoping I have to buy dinner sets and stuff for my unit. I can apply for a centre link advance and buy myself some stuff. $500 would help a lot with setting my bachelorette pad up nice. I want to get a black dinner set. I reckon they look classy. Never had one but I've seen them in the shops. In fact, whatever I get will be my first dinner set ever, how exciting.

Ha-ha, I'm growing up, I'm excited by a dinner set. Oh my god, I just realised I'll be able to buy sheets and so many other things also. Ornaments and photo frames. Who would I frame though?

I lost all my friends when I went into foster care. I never got to stay at the same school, but that I think was a good thing. I'd have to explain to people otherwise why I'm not at home anymore.

Maybe I could look at getting counselling too. I was supposed to have it in the foster home. My foster mum said I wasn't any more special than the others and she didn't have time to take anyone to counselling. Tyler said I didn't need it either. I'm just thinking though maybe I could get some answers to all the whys in my head. Or learn to live with them somehow.

Getting sleepy now, too much thinking; I'm exhausted.

Chapter 13
Draino

My alarm goes off at 4:00 am. I so don't want to get out of bed, but I want to also. Bit exciting that I have a first day at work. Wish I wasn't so exhausted though.

I make myself a coffee, first of all, I need it and a couple of cigarettes before I bother going to look for stuff. Glad I got up a bit early, but I also have to walk to the building site, so I haven't got too much time to chill. Wonder how Abbigail went last night without me at the hospital.

I'll come home after work and have a shower before I go up to the hospital. The weather's warming up and I have no doubt I'll stink after work.

I accidentally drop the spoon and it clatters to the floor; shit, I hope I don't wake Darren.

He was telling me about the job he got, but it's more like an office job. I'm really happy for him.

I want to save as much money as I can. Maybe one day I can take Abbigail away for a holiday or buy us a home or something. I want to get my license too and a car. My employment agency told me that they would help me pay for a license and driving lessons because it makes it easier for me to maintain employment. I'm just lucky at the moment the building site is so close to home.

If I stay with the company, however, the next job may not be so close.

I have so many bags to sort through to find clothes and boots, I know they're somewhere. Found. Awesome. I head for a shower after I finish my coffee.

Twenty minutes later I'm out the door. It's 5:20 am so I've still got enough time to get there. I wrack my brain, to remember who I'm to ask for. Hmmm, Will. That's right! I'm shocking with names.

I find Will. He's not as old as I thought he would be for a foreman. He must be about thirty-five. He's got blonde hair and blue eyes, but he doesn't look like a pretty boy. He looks a bit gruff and has a beer belly.

"Hi," says Will, "You must be my new labourer."

"Yeah, I reckon I am, I'm Johnny," I say.

"Excellent. Ten minutes early too, that's what I expect if you want to keep the job. We start with a toolbox meeting." He says. "I'll have a talk to you after the meeting and explain what you need to do. First though for the induction."

We go over to the office and he photocopies my white card and 18-plus card. He explains how payroll works and that I'll have to bring my birth certificate, for right to work in Australia purposes. I know it's amongst all my stuff somewhere. I'll have to find it when I get home from the hospital or I'm not allowed to work tomorrow. I've also got to find my tax file number. I think I've saved it in my phone as a phone number. I'll check it later. I do the induction and we head off to the toolbox meeting.

Fifteen minutes later, I'm back listening to Will explain what he wants me to do today.

"Have you got a hard hat?" says Will.

"Nah I don't, I have to get one this afternoon; is there a spare for today?"

"Yeah, no worries, I have a spare here. You'll need to get your own though, but it can wait till payday." I feel relieved at that news because I'm not sure I can make it to the employment agency and then workwear shop to get one.

I've only got three days till payday. Stoked at that news. I really want to buy a present for Abbigail as a housewarming gift. Sort of to say I'm sorry as well because I let her get beaten up by Tyler. I'll never forgive him, there's no excuse for hitting women. Not to mention the fact that Abbigail's only sixteen.

I never stood back and let my mum get beaten. I wouldn't stand back and let anyone else get beaten either. I really regret not doing something when he slapped her twice.

I don't know how I'm ever going to make it up to her.

I'm grateful she's forgiven me though.

So hard hat on, I walk into the construction zone and start loading bricks in the wheelbarrow for the bricklayers. I have a list of stuff to do, I'm feeling really pumped. I use all the energy I'd like to kick Tyler's ass with, to get me through the day. At lunchtime, I sit with the other fellas and one starts up a conversation with me. His name is Tre. He's from South Africa originally, but he's been here for ten years. He seems like a pretty cool fella. Lunch goes quickly though and it's back to the grind.

Before I know it, it's 3:00 pm and we're packing up the tools. The fellas invite me to the pub for a few beers, but I decline. I gotta get home and shower to go up and see Abby. She will be waiting. Two hours later I walk into her hospital room, smiling. She's eating her dinner. They serve it so early in hospitals. I suppose they serve it at the most-healthiest time to eat it, so you're not sleeping on a full stomach.

Abbigail looks up from her plate at me and gives a wonky grin. Obviously glad to see me. I'll feel better when she looks like her beautiful self again.

"Hey, you, how was your first day at work?" she asks.

"Yeah great thanks, how are you doing more importantly."

"Yeah good. I should be out of here tomorrow. I just have to go to housing and sign the bond loan forms, then I go meet Sandra at the unit," she replies. "Oh, are you coming over to bring my stuff to my bachelorette pad as you so kindly called it?"

She's trying really hard to smile which is great to see. I guess at the moment she has a lot to look forward to, which is great. Really great.

"Yep, I will be, after work tomorrow. You're going to have to text me the address."

"Yeah, no worries, I will," she says. "I'm so excited."

"I bet you are," I say. "I'm really happy for you."

"Do you ever think about what it could have been like if we had better families?"

"Ahh princess, no point worrying about stuff like that. It is what it is, never more and never less."

"Yeah still, I wonder you know."

"Me too sometimes, but you can't unpack and live off what-ifs. It'll screw your head up quicker than anything."

"Yeah, you're right, Johnny."

“We still got a lot of positive things to look forward to,” I say to Abbigail.

“That we do,” she says.

She looks deep into my eyes like she’s searching for something. I return the look and we sit here staring at each other for a while. Deep in thought, then a nurse walks in.

“Visiting hours are over,” she states.

“Thanks,” I say and get up to leave.

Abbigail grabs my hand and says, “Thank you.”

“What for?” I say.

“Everything, Johnny.”

“Don’t sweat it,” I tell her. I kiss her hand goodbye and go to leave. I take one last look back and then, I’m gone. Short walk to the train station, and I’ll be on my way home.

Chapter 14
Abbigail

I must have dozed off straight after Johnny left. Next thing I know, it's morning already and I'm getting discharged today.

Nervous as anything, feeling anxious. I think I'd be shit scared though if Tyler never got six months. I'd be worried he'd follow me from the hospital to home.

I have to sort through my stuff to find some clothes. The ones that I came in; my sundress is covered in blood and I've been wearing hospital gowns in here.

Need to find something clean that will slip over my head easily enough, without knocking my nose. Thank god it's not winter.

I take myself off for a shower and get organised to leave. The social worker said they'll give me a cab-charge voucher to get to housing.

Then I've just got to get from housing to the unit.

The dole office gave me a crisis payment they have for domestic violence victims. I didn't know about it. The social worker told me all about it and got me the supporting paperwork. I'll catch a cab from housing to the unit, so I don't have to carry all my belongings on the train. It'll also make sure I'm there on time to meet Sandra. I can't believe I'm getting a set of keys for my own crib. I'm so excited. I'm not feeling confident enough to go out shopping looking like this though, I'm feeling very self-conscious with all the bruising on my face.

In housing, the forms are signed and off I go to the unit. When I get there, Sandra is early, and she is there waiting for me.

I am absolutely gob-smacked. It's a nice dark brick unit block three stories high. There're landings on one side of the building attached to the stairs. Then there are verandas on the other side, individual ones for each unit.

"How fucking lucky am I?!" I say to myself out loud.

Sandra walks up to me and shakes my hand.

"It's a pleasure to meet you Abbigail. Have you got some paperwork about the bond loan with you?"

"Hi Sandra, yes I do, they're just in my bag." I reach down to pull them out of my bag and my head starts throbbing. I must be due for painkillers.

Well, that's OK because I'm home sweet home.

"Ready to go see your new home, Abbigail?" says Sandra with a big grin. She knows I'm going to love it.

"For sure," I say. Smiling myself, I'm just not sure my smile is as obvious.

We go up to the second level of the units and halfway across number 8.

So, my new address is 8/23, Hope Street, Toombul. Hahaha, I will have to text Johnny and let him know.

Sandra hands me the key and I stick it in the lock. So excited, I open the door and gasp. Oh my god, it is gorgeous.

There's also a bunch of flowers in a vase. I walk straight over to them and have a smell. Beautiful.

The kitchen benches are an orange colour, the carpet is brown, and floorboard-like linoleum in the kitchen, bathroom and laundry.

I love it. I open up the glass sliding doors and stand on the veranda.

Smiling as big as I can, I turn around and Sandra is behind me, smiling as big as I'd like to.

"Want me to show you around or would you prefer to do it alone?" she asks.

"No, you can show me," I say.

We start in the kitchen. Look through all the cupboards they have only the basic here. If I want anything specific, I'll have to buy it. I will make a list later on what I want for here. Then I will prioritize it and my savings.

Next is the bedroom and it's awesome. A double bed to myself, nice. Plenty of cupboard space.

"The hall cupboard has some linen. We do prefer you buy your own when you can. Saves the emergency linen for the next emergency resident."

The bathroom has some travel-size toiletries; great I can put off shopping until tomorrow.

There's an orange cupboard in the laundry with towels in it, sheets, pillowcases and face washers also.

The lounge room has a TV and DVD player. A little stereo sits on the side table. The couch is purple and white vinyl, I love it. I turn to Sandra with tears in my eyes, I'm still too sore to wipe them away.

"Thank you, you have no idea how much this means to me," I say.

"Oh, I think I have a hunch," she says as she smiles.

"I'll leave you to settle in. We will be in touch in the next few days. In the meantime, if you need anything don't hesitate to let me know."

"Thank you once again, Sandra."

"Bye, Abbigail."

As soon as she leaves, I grab my phone from my backpack and start to text Johnny. He's still in my phone as Draino, I should change that.

Me: Hi Johnny hope work is well I'm at the new crib.

The address is 8/23 Hope Street Toombul.

It's only a few minutes later I get a text back.

Johnny: Hey good to hear from you thanks I'll be there after work.

What's it like?

Me: Hey you're supposed to be working, it's good.

Johnny: It's lunchtime. Chill lol.

Me: Oh, OK that's OK then perfect timing.

Johnny: Yep, great to hear from you I should be finished by about 3 again. Gotta go home shower change and grab your stuff see you about 5.

Me: OK no worries.

I've got about five hours to kill. The walls are very white, it looks like they have just been repainted, but the room doesn't smell like paint, thank god. I don't think I could stand the irritation to the nose at the moment.

I go get a glass out of the cupboard, give it a quick rinse and have some water. I need some painkillers. The hospital made sure I had paracetamol and ibuprofen to bring with me. I take two of each as they are both overdue.

I lay down on the couch and rest my eyelids.

Chapter 15
Draino

I get to Abbigail's and there's no lights on inside her unit, I can feel my heart beating just that little bit faster. I'm excited to see her but nervous; because of the lack of lights. I knock on the door and hear a slight squeal. I call out, "Abbigail, it's me."

"Oh, thank god, just a second!" she yells back. It doesn't take long and she is answering the door.

"Hey, how are you? How was work?"

"Yeah fine, so this is the new crib, huh?" I say smiling.

"Yeah, this is home sweet home."

"Wow, it's kind of big. You have a veranda too?"

"Yeah, just a little one. I want to buy myself some paints and brushes and stuff; do some paintings to brighten up the walls. I'll be able to do it out on the veranda it'll be awesome."

"Sounds like a plan," I say. "I like it, it's bright with all the different colours, looks awesome. Love the couch too, that is a gem."

"Yeah, it's awesome, hey."

I look at Abby and she's looking back at me. I smile.

"Here's all your stuff, do you feel like going and getting some dinner?"

"Where do you want to go? I don't really feel up to being out in public."

I cringe inwardly. I feel like the biggest idiot, of course, she doesn't feel like going out in public.

I wouldn't either, all bruised and beaten.

"How about I go get some Chinese food or something across at the food court and I'll bring it back."

"That sounds great, thanks, Johnny."

"All right," he says with a smile.

When I return, Abby has some plates out ready to eat. We put some music on softly and sit down to eat. Ed Sheeran is playing "Thinking out loud."

"Last day of work tomorrow for the week," I say to Abbigail.

"So, you get weekends off, that's a good job, Johnny."

"Yeah, I reckon so too," I say. "Have you got any plans for the weekend?"

"Nah, not yet. I was thinking I'd like to go shopping but I'm hoping the bruising goes down a bit more."

She tells me about the payment for domestic violence victims she got. She also tells me about having to buy some linen and stuff for the crib. We have a big conversation and it's getting late. I'm lucky I have two days off after tomorrow. God knows I need them as it's been a full-on week, that's for sure.

"I get paid tomorrow," I say. "I have to get a hard hat for work, a few bits and pieces. I should be able to start saving up." I say with a smile.

"Yeah true, that's awesome," she replies. "I'm still hoping I get the job at Hungry Jacks. I got to contact the school too and see what I have to do to get in for next year."

"Yeah, you should be able to get their number on google and make some enquiries, even though you don't want to leave the house yet."

"Good point Johnny, I could do that tomorrow. I'm really nervous, or anxious. Not quite sure what to call it really. Everything's changed in the matter of a week, it's been crazy."

"Not wrong," I say. "It'll settle down again Abby, and everything will be better than before."

"You promise?" she says to me and I balk. How can I make a promise like that? I'm not sure what the future holds for us but giving up hope won't help; it'd just make it worse. So, I say, "I can't promise Abby, but I can promise I will stand by you no matter what. I can promise you; I will do everything I can to help smooth over the bumps in life. I can promise I'll be here for you as long as you let me. And I can promise I'll never do anything to hurt you."

She has tears running down her face again, and I'm not sure if they're happy tears on not.

"Thanks, Johnny. You have no idea what that means to me."

She looks at me like she's deep in contemplation of the future.

"You OK, Abbigail?" I ask.

"Yeah, I'm OK, Johnny. You know I don't want a relationship, though right?"

"Yeah, I know Abby, you got a lot of soul-searching to do before we even think about that. We can still hang out and be best friends, though right?"

I say smiling but feeling so uncertain.

"That'd be great, Johnny." And she is smiling too.

"Excellent." I sigh with relief.

I need to get home to bed but I still don't want to leave. I'm going to have to though, I have to remember the bigger picture and I have a hard day of manual labour to do.

So, I say good night, giving Abbigail a hug. I can feel my whole body relax into hers and it feels like home. I don't want to let go knowing damn well I have no choice.

"Night, Princess."

"Yeah, good-night, Johnny, will I see you tomorrow?"

"You can count on it."

Chapter 16
Abbigail

Johnny just left and I feel so alone, but that's a good thing. I think.

His cuddle was awesome. I didn't want to let go but he's right I have a lot of soul-searching to do. I don't need to be feeling like I have to take everyone else's feelings into consideration. Not yet anyway.

I'm just worried that if we got into a relationship, he would change just like Tyler did.

I think counselling would be a good idea, Sandra said there are people that can help with that and that I could go to Headspace. There's one at Nundah which is awesome. I just have to go get a mental health care plan Sandra said. The hospital suggested I go to the doctors anyway and ask to go on the pill, so I don't end up pregnant again before I'm ready. I have to go have a check-up too. Guess I'll have to book a long appointment.

It's getting really late and I have a couple of things to do tomorrow before Johnny comes over after work. I'll go have a shower take some pain relief and go to bed. Tomorrow is another day.

I wake around 9:00 am. I can't believe I slept in. I must say I really like my new bed, it is so comfortable, much better than Tyler's. I have no food here but there are complimentary coffee satchels, so I make myself a coffee.

I really have no choice but to go get some food. I want to get it before Johnny comes over too, so I can cook him dinner. I wonder if I could put some make-up on, but I have a feeling it would hurt too much.

By 10:30 am I'm walking out the door to go to the Toombul Centro. I've got no shopping bags, but I can buy some at Aldi. I wonder if they have any sheets or doona covers on special this week. Sometimes they do.

I've decided I'd like white sheets with plain colour doona covers and pillowcases. I also want to get six pillows for my bed. I love pillows to cuddle into. Some scatter cushions for the bed and couch would be nice too. I have to make sure I save money for uniforms, textbooks, etc.

I'm only going to get the bare essentials today though, I'm not up for a full-on shop.

At Aldi, I grab what I need to get me through for a few days, I don't have the energy to carry too much back. Then I head home.

I found a sketchbook to doodle in at Aldi to form some ideas for paintings. The pencils I bought are all different grades too. They had charcoal pencils as well, so I bought them. Why not, anyway, it will be fun to experiment.

When I get home, I text Johnny. He should be on lunch.

Me: Hi Johnny.

Johnny: Hey princess, how'd you sleep?

Me: like a log I've never had such a comfortable bed.

Johnny: Very good, I crashed big time myself. What are you up to?

Me: I've just got back from Aldi, oh btw want to come over for dinner?

Johnny: Sure, I'll be there by 5.

Me: All good, dinner will be about 6.

Johnny: Want me to grab some stuff on my way.

Me: Nah all good I got what I need. If you want a drink or something though grab one on the way.

Johnny: No worries, you don't mind if I have a beer? Do you want a drink?

Me: Nah I'm OK thanks anyway.

Johnny: OK I better get back to work.

Me: See you at 5.

Now that's sorted I pack away all the groceries and make myself some toast for breakfast. It still hurts a bit to chew, so lucky it's just got vegemite on it.

I make another coffee and take it out on the veranda with a chair to sit on, my sketchbook and pencils I bought in hand.

It's a beautiful day. I sit down and start sketching a woman's face. Then I sketch a little girl sitting on a park bench alone. She looks sad though, I'm not sure if I like that one. I hear a knock on the door and look down to my phone. It's 5:05pm. It'll be Johnny.

I go and open the door; it is indeed Johnny. I'm smiling and so is he.

"Hey, you, how was work?" I say.

"Yeah good, Princess, better now it's over and I'm here though."

"How was your day? What did you get up to?"

"Yeah good. Time got away from me, I was outside sketching right up till you knocked on the door."

"Oh, I hope I didn't interrupt. Did you want to go finish the sketch?"

"Nah Johnny, I've been at it for hours, need a break anyway."

"OK," he says.

Johnny comes in, puts his six pack of beer in the fridge, minus one as he cracks it open. Taking a swig of beer then turning to me and saying, "So, can I have a look at your sketches?"

"Umm, I guess so; they're not very good though. Well, I don't think they are."

I go out to the veranda and grab my sketchbook. Bringing it back in, I hand it to Johnny. Opening on the first page, he stares at it for a long time and my tummy is doing somersaults thinking he's not going to like it.

"Fantastic," he says. "Who is it?"

"No one that I know of, just a figment of my imagination," I say.

"I like your imagination." He smiles. "She's very pretty, like you."

"Thanks, I guess." I laugh.

I am certain I'm blushing big time. He certainly knows how to make me feel good about myself, despite everything that has happened.

"You're a good bloke, Johnny," I say. "Thanks for being there for me through this. I don't think I could've done it by myself."

"Ah babe, I have no doubt you would've been fine without me, and no matter what happens, you're a survivor. You will make it through anything."

I'm flattered that he thinks so, but I don't believe it. Not for a second.

"Well I'm going to start cooking, you hungry?" I ask.

"Starving," he replies with a smile, patting his stomach.

I laugh. Still a boy at heart.

I grab some potatoes out of the fridge, as well as zucchini and pumpkin.

I'm cooking sausages and veggies for dinner. It's only really basic, but it's all mushy and easy for me to eat at the moment. I'm going to mash the potato and pumpkin together. Cut the zucchini into four pieces and boil it but not for too long. I don't like it too soggy.

Together we find the saucepans and a frying pan to cook dinner.

Chapter 17
Draino

Abbigail's cooking dinner and I'm trying to be helpful. I'm not sure if I'm succeeding or whether I'm just in her way. She's not complaining, so I keep trying to help. I take another swig on my beer and turn to look at her. She looks deep in thought and it doesn't look pleasant.

"Are you OK?" I say.

"Yeah, I'm fine, just a bit of throbbing in my face. I guess when I was sketching, I forgot to take painkillers."

My stomach drops.

"Want me to do this, you can go sit down if you want."

"Nah, I'll be OK. I'll just take some in a tic. I just want to get the veggies on first is all."

"OK," I say.

We go silent for a minute. I put the potatoes she's cut in the biggest pot and add the pumpkin. That's how she used to do it all the time. I'm assuming it hasn't changed.

"Thanks," she says, and I'm glad I was right in my assumption.

I finish my first beer and go to grab a second. I turn to Abbigail and say, "Would you like a beer or half a beer? I bought some lemonade in case you'd like a shandy?"

She laughs, “What is a shandy?” she says.

“Oh my god,” I say. “Have you never had a shandy?” I laugh.

“Umm, no,” she says, “But I’m guessing it has something to do with beer and lemonade?”

“Yep, it most certainly does. It’s half beer, half lemonade,” I say.

“Sure, I’ll try it,” she replies.

So, I pour her a shandy in a tall glass. It won’t be enough to make her drunk. That’s not the plan.

She has a tiny sip.

“Hmm, not bad,” she says.

I go over and turn some music on just for background noise, it’s very soft. I’ve got it tuned in to the radio station Abby likes; the current song playing is Royal by Lorde. Abbigail looks at me with a big grin, this is her favourite song.

“Oh babe, please turn that up!” she says.

And I do, but she called me babe. I’m thinking it was a slip of the tongue, but I’m hoping otherwise. I say nothing but I grab her hand. I lead her over to the lounge room floor and give her a twirl. She’s cacking herself laughing. I keep up the occasional twirl and sway with her to the beat. I’ve never felt so free. I don’t think I’ve seen Abby so alive, it makes me laugh out loud. This is a memory I will never let go of.

Not even dementia in sixty years could spoil this moment, it’s frozen in time.

All of a sudden, the song ends and we can hear the spuds boiling over.

“Oops shit,” I say. I jog over to the kitchen and tilt the lid, turning the front burner down at the same time. I look at Abby sitting on the floor and my chest tightens. She is just so beautiful and the light shining through the glass doors gives her a magical glow. I take my phone and snap a photo.

Her face is turned toward the glass door, with her arms wrapped around her knees. I can imagine if she wasn't in so much pain her head would be leaning on her knee. It's something I've seen her do for the last six months. You would never guess how many times I just sat back and watched her when she was with Tyler. It hurt to watch them together, but I'm a believer in all good things come to those who wait. And I am still waiting and will forever, even if it takes that long. They say everybody has that one special person for them and Abbigail has made it to my heart like no one else could. She turns to look at me, I give a little smile and turn back to the veggies on the stove.

Dinner is almost ready. Abbigail comes up behind me, she pokes me in the ribs and says, "I was supposed to be cooking."

"Oh well," I say. "It's almost done. Where are the plates and stuff?"

"Not sure," she says laughing.

"Have you got a masher?"

"Crap, I didn't check."

I open the second drawer in the kitchen, thank god there's a masher.

I open the top drawer and get out some cutlery. Meanwhile, Abby is getting the plates.

After dinner, I start the dishes. Abby comes up and grabs the tea towel ready to dry.

"Well, I'll be," she says still laughing. "I had no idea you knew how to wash up."

"Umm yeah I do, I'm insulted." I pretend to pout.

She's still laughing at me, it's such a beautiful sound. But I can't just let her laugh at my masculinity, so I flick her with dishwater.

"Oh, like that is it?" she says laughing.

"Umm not sure what you're talking about!" I laugh. I think I'm in trouble.

"You'll keep," she says. The smile fading.

"Hey are you, OK?" I say.

"Yeah, I'm OK," she says with a weak smile.

I'm worried, but I don't want to push her into talking. Not if she doesn't want to. I'm fairly confident she will talk to me when she's ready.

After the dishes I have another beer, we sit down on the veranda to drink it.

"So, tomorrow is Saturday. Do you have any plans?" I ask her.

"Not yet, but I was hoping you'd come with me to do some shopping."

"Yeah cool, what are we shopping for?"

"I need to get some sheets and stuff for the bed, and some more food I just grabbed enough stuff for a few days."

"OK no worries. We can do that," I say. "What time do you want to do that?"

"Hmm, not sure. About ten-ish I reckon, maybe eleven. I think you need a sleep-in, Johnny. You've been going flat out for days."

I think she's right too. I could use a good sleep-in.

It's getting late and I know I need to go home but I'm wishing I didn't have to. I finish my cigarette and beer and turn to Abby.

"I better get going and let you get some sleep, Princess."

"Yeah, I guess," she replies frowning.

"What's the frown for?" I ask.

"Huh? Oh, nothing. You better get going, get some beauty sleep," she laughs. OK, that's much better. And I'm heading for the door. Abbigail follows me and opens the door to let me out.

"Thanks for the dinner," I say, feeling unsure whether I could give her a hug or not. She reaches out for a hug and I lean in. I can smell her hair it smells like apples. It feels like home, damn every time.

I don't want to let go but I know I have to. I lift my head, give her a kiss on the forehead.

"See you tomorrow."

"Yeah, see you tomorrow, Johnny."

Chapter 18
Abbigail

Johnny just left, and I'm contemplating my feelings for him. A couple of times tonight, I found my heart aching for more. I know I'm not ready for it but my feelings toward him are growing. I'm not sure what to do about it. So, I won't do anything, not yet.

I brush my teeth and hair and get ready for bed. Tomorrow is another day and I'll be spending time with Johnny.

****

I wake up at about 8 am, heading straight to the kettle to turn it on. I need my morning coffee. While the kettle is boiling, I go put the radio on. I love music, it's like the soul of life. Without music there is nothing, but deathly silence.

I wish I had a laptop or computer to search about the school, but all I have is my phone. I've decided on Monday, I will enquire about enrolling for next year. I go to the bathroom and look in the mirror, while I'm washing my hands. The bruising is fading. It's almost a yellow. Hopefully, in a few more days, it will be gone entirely.

I sit down on the veranda to drink my coffee, it's a beautiful day outside already.

I'm going to have a shower soon and find something to wear to go shopping. I might try to put some makeup on too now my face isn't so sore. It'll be good to look normal again. My nose is still very swollen, but I don't think it will be noticeable with makeup on. I find a nice pink shoe-string strap dress to wear and head to the shower.

It's so refreshing, I let the water glide over my body for quite a while. I wash my hair with my apple shampoo and conditioner before I get out.

After I get dressed, I put my hair up to keep it out of the way while I do my makeup. Foundation goes on first, then mascara. I use a white colour eyeshadow, so it's a subtle look. With a pale pink lipstick. Done. Wow even I can't believe how I look right now. The bruising isn't visible; it's almost like I forgot what I look like. Now I get my blow dryer out and dry my hair. Finally, I'm ready. It's still only 10:00 am, so Johnny should be here soon. I'm not going to text him though, in case he's still asleep.

I pick up my sketchbook and pencils, heading toward the veranda. I turn the music up a notch on my way past the stereo.

My phone tings it's a text message from Draino, still have to change his name in my phone.

Johnny: Morning Princess.

Me: Heya you managed to sleep in I'm guessing.

Johnny: Yeah, I just woke up lol.

Me: OK good, you must have needed it.

Johnny: Yep no doubt. I will get ready soon,

so, we can go shopping. Are you all organised?

Me: Of course lol, I've been up for hours.

Johnny: OK princess, see you in about an hour. X

Me: No worries see you then.

I pick up my sketchbook and head back on to the veranda. I want to put some finishing touches to my last sketch.

Before I know it, Johnny is knocking on my door. I get up and go answer it.

I answer the door and Johnny's mouth drops open.

"You look absolutely gorgeous," he says.

"You can close your mouth, Johnny." I laugh.

He closes his mouth and smiles, it's a cute smile he's wearing.

"OK, do you want a coffee or a cold drink before we go?" I ask.

"Nah," he says. "We could get a Frappuccino from the coffee club."

"Oh yum, that sounds good," I say as I grab my bag to walk out the door.

At Toombul Centro, we go to the coffee club first, grab our Frappuccino's and sit at a table. The conversation flows easily, and I feel like we are really getting to know each other. Away from Tyler and Brian, Johnny is a new man. It's not just that he's gotten a job, but he seems to have softened a bit like he was always showing a front, in front of the boys. I don't know what it is exactly, but I like the new Johnny.

I feel more comfortable in the shopping centre today than I did the other day; the makeup helps a lot, I think.

"So, where are we going first?" Johnny asks.

"I was thinking K-mart," I say. "I want to get sheets and doona covers."

"OK, let's head there then," he replies.

About two hours and three hundred dollars later, we are walking back to my unit. When we get home, I hand Johnny a beer leftover from last night and start unloading the groceries. After I put the groceries away, I turn to Johnny; he's looking at my sketchbook.

"This looks great," he says.

"Thanks," I say. "Groceries are away, do you feel like some lunch?"

"Hmm, nah, I'm good. Just make something for yourself." He smiles.

"OK, I'm not hungry at the moment though."

"I was thinking do you want to go to a movie tonight?" says Johnny.

"Yeah, that sounds awesome," I reply.

"Sweet, I'll book the tickets online now. Is there anything, in particular, you'd like to see?" Johnny asks.

"Nah, you decide. I'm not even sure what's playing at the moment."

"OK sure."

"I might go home and freshen up. I'll text you with the details, and let you know what time I'll pick you up; if that's OK, Princess."

"OK, no worries."

Johnny left and I take the opportunity to unpack the rest of the shopping.

It's pretty exciting buying the first sets of sheets ever. I've also never owned any scatter cushions, I got a red, green, yellow and orange. I reckon they are going to look fantastic on the purple and white couch. It's almost a gay pride flag right here to sit on. I'm pretty proud of that fact.

I've decided to do some more sketches while I wait for Johnny to text.

I start with an angel-type woman, she's very pretty. She doesn't have a halo, but I don't believe all angels do. I swear, there's a guardian angel watching over me from somewhere.

I'm stunned by how much my life has changed in the last week or so. It's craziness.

Trying to work out what I want to do after I do year twelve. I'm wondering seriously if university could be an option. Maybe I could get a scholarship or something. If I like, try really hard and get great marks at school; maybe a door will open somewhere.

I'm not gonna stress too much about it but I've still got three years of high school to do. I'm wishing it was Monday already so that I could go to the school and sort enrolment out. It'll be awesome. Then I can start buying stationery and stuff so I'm not forking it all out in one fortnight.

My phone rings, I don't recognise the number. I answer it anyway.

"Hello," I say.

"Hi, is this Abbigail Smythe?" asks the caller.

"Yes, this is. Who is this?"

"Hi, it's Timothy Rogers from Brisbane Correctional Centre, we have a prisoner here by the name of Tyler Stuart. He's given us your number as he would like to talk to you."

"I don't want to hear from him and there is a domestic violence order in place."

"Oh, I'm sorry. Yes, he won't be able to contact you. Sorry for wasting your time."

"OK, bye," I say.

OK, that was upsetting, what the hell. Why would they call me? Can they not see there is an order in place?

It's Saturday so I don't think there is anyone at the Domestic Violence Action Centre. I'll text Johnny.

Me: Hey Johnny the prison just rang me.

Johnny: What the hell???

Me: Apparently Tyler asked them, to put me on his call list.

Johnny: Can they do that with the dvo?

Me: I told them there's a dvo and they said I won't hear from him. But it's still upsetting.

Johnny: Yeah of course it would be. I'll come back now.

Me: you can do what you need to do first.

Johnny: I'll see you in ten minutes.

Chapter 19
Draino

Oh, my goodness, I'm fucking furious. How in the hell do the prison not know; there is a domestic violence order for Abby's benefit?

Aren't all the government files linked! I don't understand why they even tried to call Abbigail. I turn around on the footpath and head back toward Abbigail's place. I'm really worried this has upset her. The government system has a lot to answer for, I swear. I don't get how they did not know the victim's name or why he is in prison. Like seriously.

I only get another five minutes down the road, when Abby texts me.

Abby: Don't worry about coming back, I'm fine.

Me: I'm on my way, Abby.

Abby: No, I said.

OK, so I'm thinking now I need to back off and give her the space she needs, despite the fact; I really want to be there for her.

Me: OK I understand, still want to catch a movie later?

Abby: Can we give it a miss?

Me: Yeah, no worries, see you tomorrow after work?

Abbigail: Great see you then.

So, I turn around again and head toward mine and Darren's crib.

It's getting late afternoon and I have work tomorrow. I still have to do my washing for work. Damn, I forgot about that.

I'm supposed to get a hard hat too. Damn, I've been distracted. I want to dedicate so much time to Abbigail, I'm forgetting to do what I have to.

I am going to have to get into a better routine, I'm thinking. When Abbigail starts school, it will be easier because she won't have as much free time.

Between classes and homework, I wonder what she wants to do after she finishes year twelve. I'll have to ask her.

I head straight for the workwear store. Thank god they are still open. I grab a lightning-looking dark blue hard hat because it's pretty friggin awesome. I look around for some more work clothes. I find a couple of shirts and some thicker socks. Much better with steel cap boots.

It's kind of exciting buying myself new work clothes, I had a few things before, but no job to go to.

I head off to Bargain City back at Toombul Centro, I want to buy paints and stuff for Abbigail. As a surprise, I grab some large and small canvases. I grab the primary paint colours, red, blue and yellow, the shades white and black. From those colours she can make every colour. I grab a tube of brown umber as well, it's hard to make. I grab some different-sized paintbrushes and a palette and head to the counter. If I hadn't grabbed so much already, I'd buy an easel too, but I priced them while I'm here. Forty-seven dollars isn't too bad, I'll grab one next week.

I'm not going to take it back to Abbigail today, she wants some time alone. I've grabbed a bit much to walk to Nundah with, so I walk to the taxi rank.

There're a few cabs there waiting for a fare so I'm in luck. I jump in the first one and give them Darren's address. At home, I chuck a load in the machine. Darren's not home at the moment so I have the place to myself. I grab my phone and hook the Bluetooth up to his stereo.

I put on YouTube and play a Rudimental song called *These Days*. I grab the vacuum out and start cleaning. I'm not afraid to admit I do like a clean house. I'm also prepared to put in the hard work to get it there. I get some veggies and steak out for dinner. I'll cook for Darren too, even though I have no idea where he is or when he's coming home.

Next on the YouTube channel is *Lorde Royal*.

Abby loves that song so much.

I remember swinging her around her living room not two days ago. I smile at the memory and swing my hips a little. Darren walks in the door and laughs at me.

"Did you get laid or something," he laughs.

"No," I reply. "I'm just happy," I say with the biggest grin.

He laughs at me.

"Dinner will be ready soon."

"Ah, domesticated, nice one." He is cackling at me. This is so not funny.

"Get stuffed," I say in return.

After dinner I put my washing in Darren's dryer, I'll have to make sure I start paying money off the electricity bill. It'll be ready by the morning. Time to do the dishes and have a shower.

After the house is clean, I think about texting Abby. Not sure if I should give her more space or not.

I decide to ring her instead then I'll be able to tell just how chatty she is.

Her phone is ringing.

"Hey, Johnny," she answers.

"Hey you, how are you feeling?"

"Yeah good thanks, I just put a load on with my new sheets and stuff."

"Good idea to wash them first," I say.

"Ha-ha, you sound so educated to domestication." She laughs.

"Are you laughing at me?" I ask.

"Yeah," she replies.

"Hmm, I'm insulted," I say.

She laughs harder, it's great to hear her happy voice I swear to god.

"Oh, I'm going to call Adam tomorrow to reschedule the interview."

"Nice one," I reply. "You got something nice to wear to the interview?"

"I was thinking a pair of jeans and a nice top, do you reckon that would be OK?"

"Yeah should be fine, it's not an office job or something."

"Excellent," she says. "Oh, my washing just finished, ha-ha, the washing machine plays music." She laughs.

I let out a laugh too.

"That's pretty cool. I'll let you go do your washing. Do you want me to come around tomorrow after work?" I ask.

"Sure, that'd be great."

I say goodbye and hang up. Yeah, she's OK. Certainly, sounds like she's OK anyway.

I settle in front of the TV for a while. Darren sits with me watching some stupid reality show.

I hear the dryer stop and think fuck it. I get up and get my clothes out of the dryer. I head for a shower and think I'll go to bed. May as well get an early night.

Chapter 20
Abbigail

I sit outside sketching, till it gets colder and dark. The girl on the park bench looks good now. I've added more detail with the charcoal pencils. I kind of like the pencils, but they smudge. I think I can buy spray somewhere to seal the charcoal, so it doesn't smudge. Artists use it with pastels too.

I make a really basic meal for dinner. It's weird not having to cook for four. I wonder how it feels for those families out there when they lose their kids. I'm sure they'd feel similar to this when cooking after the fact.

It's too late now to call Adam to reschedule the interview, I'm hoping if I just turn up tomorrow, he will be there. I think I'll get an early night; it'll make tomorrow easier. To be honest with myself, I'm feeling a bit nervous about being so public by myself. I guess it's all part of the rehabilitation process. Learning to live without fear. I still haven't unpacked all the bags Johnny bought over my first night here. Guess I should do something about it. Grabbing a few bags from the lounge I start to sort through them. There's a couple of skimpy outfits that Tyler bought me. I bin them. I never want to see them again. I find jeans and a nice shirt. If I wear that with my glittery sandals it should look good. I'm sure I saw an iron here somewhere. My clothes are all so creased from being thrown in bags. I find my diary amongst all my belongings. It gives me a wave feeling of grief over my body and mind. It doesn't last long, but I can feel the after-effects, of it happening. I feel numb as I grab the diary and throw it in the bin. I'm never keeping a diary again. Sure, it may be great to re-read the good bits, life's full of bad bits too though. They're the moments I need to let go of to keep holding strong. I'll never forget but I don't like to dwell on hard feelings. It makes me feel bad for stuff other people have done. That's not healthy.

I have to put myself first for a while, focus on creating a stable future for myself.

I remember one day when I was with Tyler, we were walking through Nundah Village and I saw a girl I was in foster care with. She must have become a junkie when we got kicked out. She had needle marks up her arms and looked skinny and older somehow. It had only been about three months but by the clothes she was wearing, I'd say she got into prostitution too. Such a sad state to be in. I felt bad, but I looked the other way when she tried to smile at me. I didn't want to have to admit I knew her once upon a time. I'm ashamed though, that I was embarrassed to know her.

It's kinda hard you know; to find where you fit into the picture of life. Especially when you've been told or shown time and again, you're not wanted.

Not by anyone. Makes it hard to belong. I find I tend to attract other kids from the same situations. The good kids you know, their parents don't want them associating with our type. So, I'm stuck hanging out with people I have nothing in common with. Well, that's a bit unfair. We have a troubled life in common, but I want my life to go well; not stay in the rut. Not everyone has that mindset of wanting to be bigger and better.

Johnny does now though I can tell, what with getting a job and all.

Maybe when I go back to school, I can meet some academic like-minds.

Might help me get an idea about what I want to do after school too.

I iron my clothes for tomorrow and head to have a shower. I need to wash the make-up off before I go to bed. I set my alarm for 7:00 am. I want to get up early and go to Hungry Jacks. Show some initiative. My foster mother used to say all the time, I need to show more initiative. If only she cared to see me now.

After my shower, I go to bed. I'm exhausted it's been a massive day. I'll wash my hair in the morning when I wake up.

Chapter 21

Draino

BLAP, BLAP, BLAP. Oh crap, it's morning, my alarms blaring at me. I roll out of bed, grateful I got an early night.

I turn it off before it wakes Darren up. I go put the kettle on.

It's too early to text Abby yet, so I browse Facebook while I drink my coffee.

I haven't got too long to sit around. I have to get ready for work. Big handful of stuff to take to work today, with my hard hat and lunch. Not to mention bottles of water; it's hot working in the sun. It'd be a lot easier if I had a car I swear.

I still have to contact my employment agency; tell them I'm working now. Hopefully, I can do it in my lunch break. I'm going to ask them about getting my license too. I'd be able to save up for a car, easy now since I'm working.

Might ask them about getting some tickets too. Hoping to one day be a foreman myself; I'm still young enough to go for it.

I finish my coffee, chuck some clothes on and head back to the kitchen again. I rustle up some meat and cheese with tomato, whip it on some buttered bread and call it a sandwich.

Chucking it into my lunchbox quickly, I head out. Only got 30 minutes to get there.

Chapter 22
Abbigail

BAAA, BAAA, BAAAA. Damn my alarm, I was really enjoying that sleep. I need to change my alarm it sounds like a sheep. I'd nearly have to say that's the best sleep I've had, ever since everything happened. I get out of bed, having to move half a dozen pillows first. I smile to myself in the mirror; looking good. Even if I do say so myself.

I look at my phone, no missed calls or messages.

So, I text Johnny.

Me: Hey you, how's work?

Johnny: I'm not allowed to text you when I'm working remember? ☺

Me: Correct get back to work! ;-)

Funny stuff. I get ready to walk out the door grabbing my house keys and backpack on the way. I shut the door and head toward the staircase.

Taking a step at a time, I walk myself to the bus stop. I'm so nervous about my first job interview. Not really sure how to calm my nerves. Maybe he won't be there and this panic would have been for nothing. Opening the door to Hungry Jacks, I walk up to the counter, I can see Adam standing there. So, I walk straight toward him.

"Hi Adam, I'm Abbigail."

"Ah yes, hi Abbigail. Have you come to see me about that interview?"

"Yes please, if the opportunity is still there?"

"Indeed, it is," he says. "Come over to this table and let's have a chat."

Walking over to the table I can feel my hands shaking, I'm making a conscientious effort to not wring my hands together.

Low and behold, the interview went off without a hitch. OMG, I start on Wednesday. That's only two days away, like fuck! I'm so excited. I'm not too sure what to do now; then it occurs to me, the school.

****

Chapter 23

Draino

A hard day's work is done, and I am seriously thinking of visiting Abbigail. I'm worried though that I'm crowding her too much, too clingy or something.

I decide to text her instead.

Draino: hey you, how was your day?

Hmm OK, no reply, maybe she's really busy.

Not even two minutes later my phone receives a message. I look at it to see that Abbigail has texted me; I can feel the relief flow through my body.

Abbigail: hey there, how are you going?

Draino: yeah good and you? It's great to hear back from you.

Abbigail: yeah cool, been a busy day, do you mind if I call?

Draino: I can do better than that, how about I come over for a while and you can fill me in on all the gossip?

Abbigail: Yeah cool, how about I put some dinner on for us?

Draino: all good, I'll bring some with me, what do you feel like?

Abbigail: KFC sounds good.

Draino: sweet. See you soon.

So, I headed off toward the train station with an extra skip in my step, so excited to be going to see Abbigail. I'll stop at the KFC around the corner from Abbigail's so it's still nice and fresh when I get there. I wanted to buy her more gifts now I'm making decent money but I'm going to try to get a car in the next couple of months. At least then if Abbigail has a late shift, which is more than likely with her going to go back to school; I can pick her up from work. I don't think it will be too much longer and Tyler will get out of prison and there will be concerns with her catching a bus or train from work.

It stresses me out, to think of what he would do to her if he could just get his hands on her one more time.

I'd never forgive myself if something happened to her.

My love for her is growing every day and I don't know if I can hold my feelings back from her for much longer.

I'd love to just propose to her and get it over and done with. I know she's the one for me but I know she is not ready for that kind of relationship. Being with Tyler has really rattled her self-confidence. It reminds me of when I first met her, she had lost a lot of confidence due to her abuse as a child and then along came Tyler, who picked her up and protected her with our help. But not now; she is rattled again. I think "Once bitten twice shy" applies here. She has lost all her confidence and it's going to take time for her to become self-reliant and trust her own instincts again. That is the ultimate goal of mine for her. She has her own ideas, and I respect that but that I hope is a mutual goal of ours.

I have to give her some space to find and achieve her own ideals, it's hard when I just want to do it for her. Though I know when I was in the same position, I had to be so self-reliant and it was pretty much a case of trust no one. I'm a simple man though, as long as I'm earning enough to support my girl, eat, have a roof over our head; with the bills paid. I'm a happy man.

So, I get to Toombul Centro and walk straight to the food court. On my way, I walk past the jewellers. I pause at the window to look at the engagement and wedding rings. Some of them have eternity rings too. I have absolutely no idea which one she will like so I make it my mission that until I work out exactly what she likes, I will not buy her a ring.

I must work out what the perfect ring will be before I buy it to propose.

Going to KFC, I order a family feast so that Abbigail has some leftover for breakfast tomorrow. Then I go to the bottle shop and get a six-pack of beer for the evening with Abbigail. I make sure I grab lemonade with the meal so I can make her a shandy again, she seemed to like that the last time. I know she's not much of a drinker but by the sounds of her texts she has a lot to tell me and I'm wondering whether she needs a bit of Dutch courage to get her words out.

I have no idea what she wants to discuss, but I'm hoping it will turn out to be a celebratory drink.

Almost there. Abbigail opens the door right before I get there. I wonder how many times she checked the doorway before I actually got there. The thought of her having any interest in me makes me feel so excited. She's wearing the biggest grin and I know straight away, that tonight is going to be a good night.

Chapter 24
Abbigail

Oh! Thank god! Finally, Johnny has arrived. I've never been so anxious to see him before and I'm wondering if I'm starting to catch feelings for him.

It's not a feeling I'm sure I know how to deal with, at the moment though so I push it aside.

If in doubt, do nothing, that is my theory. At this particular point in time, regardless of the question, I need twenty-four hours to process my feelings. Then I may be able to make a smart choice having deliberated. Sheesh! Big words. I feel so intellectual since enrolling back in school, crazy I know. I have yet to have a single lesson. Anyway looks like Johnno has arrived bearing gifts, it's almost like he knows what mood I'm in and is so accommodating; he never gets it wrong. Crazy days. So, I let him in with a swish of my hand through the doorway. He grins and I melt, internally, of course. I cannot let these things be known yet. I give a little chuckle though and say, "Hey you, how is it going?" with a big grin.

"Hey yourself, so what are we celebrating? Come on, spit it out." The grin is as big as mine, the cheek hurting material.

"HAHA! Drinks first then I'll spill, I swear."

"Hmmm, right well I guess I best get two glasses and pour," he replies. "Are you hungry, do you want me to serve you some dinner up?"

"Hmmm, not yet. Let's sit down and chat first." I state simply with the same goofy smile. Unbelievable.

Any way Johnny pours us drinks and joins me in the lounge room. I sit down on the three-seater couch and curl my legs up under me. I'm not nervous about how he will react but it kind of reminds me of telling Tyler why I wanted a job. I know they are two completely different types of people but still, what do they say about reflective instinct?

So, I'm comfortable and feel secure in my stance on the couch as I explain how I had an interview with Adam at Hungry Jacks and I start in a couple of days. I also explain how I went to the school to enrol and that I just need to get my birth certificate. All of a sudden Johnno jumps up in excitement. Once the initial shock of the sudden movement is gone, I start to giggle at his response. He's a crazy one I swear. I'm fully laughing not even a minute later, and the beers go clink as our glasses meet.

"To the future," announces Johnno and a smile spreads across my face with glistening in my eyes. I can feel the tears trying to form. Happy tears of course.

"Thank you," I state simply "For being supportive and for just being you. There is no one I would rather share this moment with than you, after all, what we've been through together, I have no doubt we've built a friendship to last the distance." And Johnno's face levels. "What's wrong," I ask quietly.

"No, no, no, nothing's wrong babe, I promise I'm so happy for you and I don't want to rush you, but I have feelings for you Abbigail. *Friends* is great though, don't get me wrong. I'm just hoping one day we can be something a bit more. I love you," he states simply and there it is.

I'm newly confused again as I am still trying to work out my feelings that are growing toward Johnno myself. I have no way to let him know what I don't know myself. I say the only thing left to… "Let's eat."

Chapter 25

Draino

OK, I think that went better than I expected, didn't it? Or did it?

I'm not sure about how that went. I know she knows how I feel but I have absolutely nothing to know how she feels and whether my feelings are one-sided or reciprocated. I'm scared to say that I feel like she feels something but that's the impression I'm getting. I don't want to rush her but it's so hard to feel like I have to hold my feelings back when she needs love and support the most. I've been in abusive relationships myself and I know how hard it is to trust again; not only other people but yourself and your own judgement. Not to mention other people's opinions on what is good for you also. So often they are wrong. I worry also that over time Abbigail isn't going to feel the same way about me that I feel about her. That she will get impatient with my insecurities and leave instead of reassuring me. I guess I still have a lot of issues to work through myself.

Just unsure of how to do it. They say time heals all wounds but does it? Or does it just numb the pain we are used to feeling every day? I'm guessing that it takes time to work it all out in your head to get on the right road to recovery.

I'm probably best concentrating on work at the moment. I've been thinking about whether I will need to take time off work when Tyler gets out to make sure that Abbigail remains safe. I just don't know what's going to happen, I feel so unsure. It's not a nice feeling. I'm so proud of her for going back to school and getting part-time work. Between that and her art at home, she's not going to have a lot of free time. That will be both rewarding and fulfilling for her though. Healing also. She has been through so many ordeals with everything that put her into foster care then put her on the streets, then in with Tyler and now.

I decide for the next couple of days I'm just going to text and call her. I'm not physically going to see her, to give her some space. If she really wants to see me in that time away, she will let me know; I am sure.

Tomorrow after work, I will go to the employment agency and fill them in on my new job and see if they can help me get my license. I'd also like to ask them about getting some tickets. Maybe I could get one for a bobcat or something.

****

The next afternoon after work, I head straight to the employment agency. I see the leggy blonde officer that I normally deal with through the window, so at least she's in. I can never remember her name though, not sure if it's Tara or Kara, maybe Lara? Bugger me. I open the door and she turns to face me, she's always so nicely dressed in heels and shit, does nothing for me I like my ladies' cosy and homely. I walk up toward her smiling and she meets me in the middle of the room.

"Hey Johnny, how are you today?" she asks.

"Hey yeah, I'm good thanks… umm?"

"Shara," she replies.

"Yeah sorry, I'm a shocker with names, but on a bright note…"

I paused. "I have good news though, I started a new job last week."

"Fantastic news!" Shara replies. "Oh, fantastic sit down and tell me all about it and we can work out what we can do to support you through it."

"Well it's on a construction site, so lucky I got that white card. I bought a hard hat already and the shirt and boots you bought me for the agency interview came in handy too," pausing I wonder what else she might want to know.

"Well, we should be able to reimburse you for the hard hat and do you need more work clothes?" Shara asks.

"Yeah, I'll need more shirts and shorts if you can. Also, the pay's $23 an hour from 6:30 am to 3:00 pm, five days a week."

"Fantastic! Wow, so excited for you, have you thought about any courses in the field to expand your knowledge?" she asks.

"Sure, I was thinking I wouldn't mind getting some tickets like my bobcat one maybe, but I really want to get a car license and car."

"Yes, most definitely. Do you have a tablet or something you can practise the test online with?"

"I only have my phone," I say.

"OK we will give you a tablet with an initial recharge voucher after that you will have to recharge the data on it yourself or you are welcome to use the Wi-Fi here in the office."

"Oh, wow! Yeah, that would be great."

"OK fantastic! So we just have to go through all this paperwork and then, you can get out of here," she says.

Half an hour later I'm walking out of there. We also called Centrelink and reported my income. I should only have to put one more form in.

I decide to get dinner on the way home and go set up this new tablet so I can start practising for my learner's test.

I grab some Indian from Nundah village and sit down at home to see what I need to do; I'm guessing it's the same process as a phone though. Coming from the fridge, back to the couch I sit down and crack the stubbie open.

Taking a swig, I wonder what Abbigail is doing?

I pull my phone out of my pocket and see I've missed a text from her.

Abbigail: Hey everything OK? I haven't really heard from you.

So, I quickly pump out a reply.

Johnny: Heya princess, sorry I called into the employment agency after work and I didn't want to text you too early, how are you?

Abbigail: Hey that's OK, glad everything is fine. I was just getting worried.

Johnny: sorry didn't mean to worry you. How has your day been?

Abbigail: yeah OK I guess, last day before I start work tomorrow.

Johnny: cool! what time do you start and finish?

Abbigail: I have a short shift so 4-8pm when it's the busiest he said.

Jonny: OK I will be there to pick you up when you finish.

Abbigail: ummm Johnny.

Johnny: yeah

Abbigail: thanks

Johnny: lol what for I haven't done anything.

Abbigail: for being you, you're awesome ☺

Johnny: Night Abbigail ☺

Abbigail: night you.

Another day down, as I fall onto the bed. I wish that I would be curling up under the doona with Abbigail. I wish I could smell her hair, even just the memory though, of how her hair smells makes mine all stand up. I grab my phone and fall asleep looking at the photo I took of Abbigail on her new bachelorette pad floor. Not all angels have halos.

Chapter 26
Abbigail

It was late when Draino left and I stopped texting. I woke up twice in the middle of the night, both times to nightmares. I was sweating so much, and I could feel my heart racing in my chest. I felt like it was going to jump out of my throat. The fear of being left alone in this world with no one but myself. It's not even like I haven't been there before but it's not like I ever want to be there again.

I love him I know I do but I have absolutely no idea what to do about it or where it could ever go. I've been the odd one out my whole life and to be brutally honest, I don't think there is ever anyone who can put up with me. The whole distorted loveable hunk of junk me. I'm odd; I mean how could I not be. Everyone I've ever been a part of has left me starting with my parents. I may have come from another world for all that it achieves having been someone before now. But I'm just not very loveable.

As the tears roll down my face in the middle of the night, I try so hard to tell myself that it's not my fault… but if we all said that then whose fault would it be? I feel like I must take responsibility for who I am. But honestly who am I? I'm not sure I know or that I am a good enough judge of character to make that kind of decision. I have absolutely no faith in my ability to judge people let alone myself and what my standards are, or what is good for me. I feel like I'm already set in my ways and that it doesn't benefit me at all. Like I try to scare people away in self-preservation mode. Can I change? Do I want to? He's working and has come so far in the last few months it's crazy; like he was waiting for the perfect opportunity to step up to the plate. I toss and turn for at least another hour before I give up and go to my laptop. I pick it up but before it even turns it on; I'm placing it back on the couch and picking up the sketchpad instead. I sketch a picture of my memory of Draino. It seems to glide off the pencil naturally; like I was made to draw him particularly. I'm starting to think I need to see a shrink. My head feels so messed up after the last few months and I don't even know how to go about sorting it out with myself. Maybe I should go see a doctor and organise to see a psychologist. I'm sure it wouldn't screw me up any worse.

It's times like this I wish I had a mum; so, I turn the page and draw myself the ideal mum, kind face, sweet smile, dark hair with pale hazel eyes.

I lay there for a while and I must have dozed off again. It's those sorts of things, I don't like to talk to anyone about. Some things are best left lying dormant, even if they're not dormant you know. I find if I talk about the bad times it makes them feel like they go for longer, but if I just keep it on the low; no one can throw it back at you or it doesn't give them power over your happiness. I don't like to acknowledge my nightmares, dreams though, I do for sure. Nightmares; nope they never hold any weight the next day. That's what I tell myself anyway. It's like 3:00 am, I know I should get some more sleep, but I get out of bed and start sketching instead. I sketch Draino, he's lying on the couch sound asleep and looking like a saint. I don't know how I ever got so lucky to have him support me through all this. He brings out the best in me, not the stress in me you know. I just wish he was here really, asleep on the couch.

I must have drifted off on the lounge room floor contemplating my next line with the pencil.

I get up and make myself a coffee, the sun is already shining so I take the coffee and my phone and go sit on the veranda chair.

I decide to ring the doctor's surgery and make an appointment for tomorrow morning. I have work this afternoon but then my next shift isn't for two days.

Once that's done I finish my coffee and go back to bed. Tiredness is too real and I need to be alert for my first shift today.

****

I wake up about 1:00 pm and freak out. I slept most of the day away. Calming down from the initial shock of the time I make my second coffee for the day.

Time to get ready for my first job ever. So nervous I'm not sure having coffee is a good idea at all. Maybe I should switch to decaf. Hmmm, thank god they supply uniforms otherwise it would take me forever to work out what to wear. My mind is whirling with a thousand different thoughts at once and I feel like I am slowly going insane. After my shower I put my hair up, put on just a smidgen of makeup, the bruising is gone now but I still want to feel good to get through the first shift. I redo my hair in two plaits, one on each side just to help keep my hair out of the way and make it easier to get into the hair net. Feeling pretty good. I get my uniform on and some black non-slip shoes the employment agency bought for me when I went in to sort out my birth certificate, both for work and school.

Twenty minutes later I'm walking out the door to get to work. Can't wait to see Johnny when he picks me up at 8:00 pm.

Chapter 27

Draino

Today has been a crazy day at work. We've been told that construction is behind schedule and we need to pick up the pace otherwise workers will have to be let go. Something to do with profit margins. I'm looking forward to a beer at the pub around the corner from Hungry Jacks. I'll go and check in on Abbigail and let her know I am close by, ready to pick her up. I wonder how her first day of work is going and whether she is enjoying it or whether she is just overwhelmed by everything she needs to learn about the job. I'm so grateful that Adam was understanding of the delay in the interview. I check the time on my phone and I'm glad we only have an hour and a half till knock-off time. Foreman calls out to me, "Draino!"

"Yeah boss," I reply.

"Need you to do some overtime if you can. Some of these fellas can't; they've got kids to deal with."

"Yeah OK, as long as I'm done by 7:30," I say. Fuck, I dread the thought of Abbigail having to get home by herself.

"Yeah, till about six we're going to work."

"OK sweet yeah, count me in."

Can't wait to see my next pay packet; I could use a little extra dosh in my wallet. I relax back into the fast pace of work knowing I'm not leaving soon. Feeling good about the overtime too, getting an extra opportunity to prove myself beneficial to the company. I have to study for my learner's test ASAP so that I don't get disadvantaged if the next job is far away.

I suppose I'm lucky that I'm in the city and we have trains and buses to get around. Don't suppose it would take any longer than driving really with the traffic so bad sometimes and all. But still, I want the best opportunity to keep working and the trains don't go everywhere here. Dunno but I reckon Abbigail is a good influence on me you know, she brings out the best in me. Like I wanna be the best me I can be for her. I hope one day I can buy us a house and stuff, maybe I could build one sometime if I learn enough working for this company. But yeah that'll be way off in the future sometime.

For now, it's just great to be getting off my ass and the dole.

Chapter 28
Abbigail

I've been working at Hungry Jacks now for about three months. It's great and I still get part payment from Austudy; homeless allowance. I only work a couple of nights a week, after school. Johnny comes and picks me up from work every shift without fail. He's buffed up a bit now with all the manual labour he does. He's fantastic really. I love the work and I made a friend as well. Her name is Sarah, she's awesome. Same age as me but she has blonde hair, she's skinny and still lives at home with her parents. But, oh my lord, she has the funkiest blue eyes I have ever seen. She invites me over to her folks all the time for dinner and just to hang out. Quite often though we just hang at my crib. I don't think her parents like her coming to mine too much though, because no adults around. She goes to school too, but not the same one as me. It's cool though because I didn't think I would meet anyone to be friends with. Like I didn't think I'd have anything in common with anyone. Yeah, Sarah is good value. She and Johnny get along well too. She calls him Draino though. She came with me to Johnny and Darren's for a movie pizza night one night, she and Darren get along great too. Her parents would flip though if anything were to happen, what with Darren being twenty and her only sixteen.

I'd have to say my favourite teacher at school though is my art teacher. She's awesome. Black curly hair with the greenest of eyes. Her name is Martha. Yeah, she's cool.

Sarah and I have plans to catch up again tonight, were going to hang out at her parents' place and work on our assignments for school. Better to do it there I guess so that her parents can see I'm not distracting her totally from her studies.

My phone rings and I look to see it's Johnny. Wonder why he's calling me while he's at work? Better answer it I guess to see what's up.

"Hello, how's work going?"

"Hmm, been better," he says. "Tyler got out today."

"For real!"

"Yeah, sucks I know but he rang asking about you."

"What did you say?"

"Said I don't know nothing."

"OK, so he hasn't got over it all yet?"

"Don't think so babe. Sorry, wish I had better news."

"It's not your fault Johnny. But fuck I was going to go to Sarahs. Study there."

"Can you wait till I finish work and I'll get you there?"

"Not sure I want to go anywhere now, to be honest, Johnny."

"OK, I'll come and see you after work anyway," he says.

I nod in response then realise he can't see me, and I shake my head at myself. I was hoping it wouldn't rattle me this much when Tyler got out, but I guess it was bound to.

"OK, I'll see you then," I eventually reply. I sit down on my couch and then slide down to the floor. I grab one of the throw cushions off the couch. I'm still on the floor in a daze hours later when I hear a knock on my door. I don't even want to know who is there, I just want to be alone for a while. Hearing Tyler is out of prison reminds me of the pain, the shame, and the baby I lost. I start to cry, and I feel the tears slide silently down my cheeks. The next minute I hear Johnny at the door, "Abbigail, it's me."

I slowly get up off the floor while I frantically wipe the tears off my face. I don't want him to see me cry.

Like mum used to always say I must hold strong you know; I gotta keep it together.

I open the door and Johnny is standing there with a bottle of scotch and two litres of coke.

"Feel like a drink?" he asks.

"Bloody oath," I reply.

"Have you been crying?"

"A little, not to worry though I guess it's to be expected, yeah?"

"Yeah I guess, come here, let me give you a hug."

I accept the hug from Johnny gratefully and I'm starting to relax now he is here. I still haven't told Johnny about losing the baby and I'm still not sure I want to. At the same time though I think it's time I got the burden of it off my chest. It's like a big elephant I'm carrying around with me.

Johnny pours us both a drink, he just guessed how much to put in. We don't have a pourer in my unit. To be honest, I'm really not a drinker but just this once it won't hurt.

We go sit on the couch. I don't think either of us feels like sitting on the veranda knowing that Tyler is out there somewhere and might see us if we're outside.

I sit back into the corner of the couch and put my feet up so I'm alone in my bubble. I take a big gulp of my drink and almost spit it back out with a cough. I never realised how strong a flavour scotch has. I guess today's the day for learning, huh. I look at Johnny and he has a worried look on his face.

"Anything you want to get off your chest princess," he says to me.

I give him a half-smile, he always seems to know the right thing to say, it never ceases to amaze me.

"I lost the baby, when Tyler beat me up," I say. "Sorry, that didn't come out right."

"Were you pregnant?" he asks and the look on his face is sad. He pales slightly as he says, "I'm sorry Abbigail, I never knew."

"Ahh, yeah well I never knew either, neither did Tyler. It was a blessing in disguise really, I'm not ready to be a mum and definitely not to Tyler's child."

I go on to explain about the fact I had to have a curettage at the hospital before they would discharge me. That I'm not sorry I lost the baby but that I'm sad that it happened with Tyler, especially with how controlling he was.

Johnny sits there and listens to me pouring my heart out for hours on the abuse I coped with at home when I was younger, how mum never stuck up for us and how I ended up in foster care. Then eventually on the streets which is where I met Tyler and consequently Draino, aka Johnny.

My phone rings and I look down, it's Sarah trying to call. I can't deal with it all at the moment I text her to say something came up and could we catch up tomorrow? She replies straight away with OK.

I start to feel very sleepy and put my head on Johnny's lap. He sits there quietly just listening to me talk myself to sleep. He strokes my hair so gently and it feels like I'm bathed in affection. I haven't had that for a very long time if ever. I'm just lapping it up.

Slowly my mumbling stops and I fall into a deep slumber.

Chapter 29
Draino

Abbigail fell asleep about half an hour ago. I've just been stroking her hair. I swear my heart broke when I found out she was pregnant with Tyler's baby. I'm not sorry she told me. I feel like we're finally getting somewhere. I move her head off my lap and stand up so I can pick her up and put her in her bed. I'm not going anywhere tonight. I go pull her doona back ready to put her in bed. As I put her in bed, she says to me. "Stay here with me, Johnny." So I do. I curl up next to her on top of the doona and she wraps her arm around me. My mind's still on high alert listening for any unexpected noises or shadows in windows, though I doubt he will be out the bedroom window on the second storey. Abbigail looks so beautiful sleeping, though she is a little restless. I slowly calm my mind enough to get some sleep and off I drift.

I wake up at the sound of a thump on the door. Freaking out thinking it's damn Tyler. Not sure really what to do until I hear a female voice say, "Police."

I get up without disturbing Abbigail for which I am grateful. I walk quickly to the door to answer it before they knock again. Worried that Abbigail will be woken to bad news and won't get any sleep.

The officer has a serious look on her face as I open the door. She asks me who I am. I answer quickly and quietly telling her that Abbigail is sound asleep, and I really don't want to wake her unless I have to.

"Hi Johnny, can I see some ID?" she asks.

I go to my back pocket and pull out my learners' permit. Handing it to the officer, I'm feeling so anxious wondering what's going on.

"Sorry about that." she replies "You're down as her next of kin from the hospital. Tyler, as you may know, was out of prison?"

"Yeah, I'd heard that," I reply.

"OK well, he was spotted by security around here drunk and disorderly. Because of this, he has breached his probation conditions and has been locked up again."

"Oh OK," I say, stunned by the officer's words.

"Because he was found in this area, he was also in breach of the domestic violence order conditions as well. We thought we would give Abbigail a courtesy visit to say he has been re-apprehended."

"Umm OK, thank you so much," I reply unsure what else to say but the sudden relief is overwhelming. I will tell Abbigail in the morning when she wakes up.

Chapter 30
Abbigail

Waking up I realise Johnny is still here, sleeping soundly on top of the doona on the bed. I want to wake him up; I don't want to be alone right now.

I just feel that this nice world I've been building for myself is going to crumble like a porcelain jug falling from the second floor. It was all falling into place and getting to the point where I felt like I was almost normal.

Like I could start dreaming of things for the future and that they may come true. Why does Tyler have to be released? I go lay back down next to Johnny and cuddle under his arm. It feels like the safest place to be at the moment. He starts to stir so I go to move away so he can go back to sleep.

"Abbigail, good morning, please don't leave," he says in a sleepy voice.

"OK, but did you want a coffee, Johnny?"

"It can wait. The police turned up early this morning. Tyler's locked up again."

"Umm OK? What happened?"

"He was found drunk not far from here, so he breached his probation conditions and also the domestic violence order."

"Wow! That close, hey?"

"Yeah, must have been security spotted him and called the police."

"So, he won't be out for a while?"

"Nope, not for a few more months. I want to go get my license so that I can drive you to and from work when he gets out again."

"That would be good for you too Johnny."

"Yeah, I reckon so too," Johnny says.

So, I get off the bed and go to make Johnny and myself a coffee and some toast with vegemite on it. Not sure about Johnny but I couldn't eat so much last night with the stress of finding out Tyler was out. The sudden relief is amazing; I can't believe how hungry I suddenly am.

I hear the toilet flush just before Johnny walks out to the kitchen.

I hand him his coffee and he says "Thanks," as we go and sit down on the couch.

I'm grateful to Johnny for the update and give him a hug as we sit on the couch.

"How much of the school essay do you have left to do?" Johnny asks.

"Hmm, quite a bit," I reply.

"Did you want me to go home so you can get organised?"

"Nah all good Johnny, I want to do some painting and stuff; de-stress before I start."

"Did you want to be left alone while you do that?"

"Actually," I smile as I say, "I would like to paint you on the couch."

"Ha-ha, are you for real?"

"Yes, indeed now you can sit however you like as long as you're comfortable. I'm just going to get everything set up."

"Um OK."

Johnny sits down on the couch as I grab a canvas and some paints, a palette and brushes.

I sit on the floor near the corner of the lounge room and get myself prepared. Carefully placing down the glass of water and paintbrushes I start making different colours I'll need for the painting. He looks nervous but I'm hoping he will relax soon and just drift away in thought. I love the look on his face when he's a million miles away.

It's very comforting when he is relaxed.

"OK, are you comfortable?" I ask.

"Are you sure you want to paint me?" Johnny asks.

"Ha-ha, yes I'm sure!" I laugh.

I start painting and I can see him relax, it's awesome how he just gets in the zone. I wish that I could do that more often when Johnny isn't around.

He makes my home feel like home.

I'm not sure what to do about my feelings so I shut them off; they can wait. I pick up the paintbrush again and work on the outline. I'm not quite sure how it's going to turn out, but I honestly think Johnny won't care.

I paint for a while and the radio is on in the background. All of a sudden another song I love comes on the radio and that's it. I put down my paintbrush and say to Johnny.

"Let's dance."

The lyrics roll off my tongue.

"I'm a bad liar, I'm a bad liar." The song by the Imagine Dragons hits home and yes; I'm a bad liar. I am fast falling in love with Johnny but I am scared of the feelings I feel. I'm not sure I can really ever admit the feelings I feel for him.

He's been my rock through one of the worst chapters of my life. I also want him to witness the best. It's pretty good at the moment, I have a job, friends and school again. Life is pretty fucking amazing.

So I paint him smiling. He always looks at me with a special glint in his eyes, it excites me as I don't think I've ever seen anyone that way looking at me. I've seen it in couples walking down the street looking at each other. Never aimed at me before though.

It's definitely a new experience. We spend about three hours just chilling and painting while Johnny talks to me about lots of different things. I get some of the background on how he came to be homeless and living with Tyler and Brian. It's sad you know but I hear it all the time. Maybe because my ass has sat in the sad state itself, I find many people who have experienced the same kinds of things.

I dunno if it's fate or whatever, that brings us together. But like minds generally find each other in this big bad world.

I dream of a better beginning and a happy ending, nothing I can do about the beginning and maybe it's not about the happy ending maybe it's about where life takes you in the middle. I want to be much more than I have been before, more enthusiastic about living, about learning and about growing mentally as an individual and as part of society. So what if I had a crummy beginning, I'm determined to not unpack and live there in the crumbs of what life has to offer.

I finish the last brushstroke of the painting and smile at Johnny.

"It's done," I say.

"Can I look?" he replies.

"Sure can."

He comes around and has a look.

"Oh my god, are you sure that's me? He's kinda good looking in that painting there."

I laugh at Johnny wholeheartedly. Unbelievable; he has no idea how good-looking he actually is.

"You up to going for lunch Johnny, I have a shift later but I don't start till 5:00 pm."

"Don't you think you should work on your essay."

"Oh, shit yeah, I forgot about that."

"OK well, how about I go get us fish, chips and salad while you work on your essay. I'll be back soon."

"Oh, shit yeah, thanks heaps Johnny. I'll leave the front door unlocked for you, I'm just going to sit up here at the table."

Johnny leaves as I go and get the books I need to read and the notepad I use for my essay notes. It makes it easier to type it up with a hard copy of the notes in front of me.

I get stuck into the texts and it all starts falling in place. I'm grateful it's on a topic I'm not completely naïve about because that makes it just that little bit easier.

Just as I'm finishing off my notes Johnny walks in with the food. Thank God it's perfect timing. I'll come home after work and type it all up on the computer. I've still got a couple of days till it's due.

Johnny gets the plates out and dishes lunch up for us.

"Thanks Johnny, much appreciated," I say with a smile. "I finished the research and note-taking."

"Wow, that didn't take long."

“Nah I’ve got a pretty good grasp on the topic and I’d already done some of the research in the school library the other day,” I say smiling.

We sit in utter silence for a while just concentrating on eating lunch.

“Aww, I’m stuffed. Thanks for lunch,” I say to Johnny.

“All good, anytime.” He smiles. “But hadn’t you better get ready for work?”

“Yeah, I probably should.”

“Want me to wait and walk you to work?”

“If you don’t mind, the company would be great.” I smile at Johnny and he goes and starts the dishes.

I quickly go jump in the shower and towel around me, I walk to the bedroom to put my uniform on. A little bit of makeup and I’m almost ready to walk out the door.

Johnny grabs his stuff and off we toddle to Nundah. At the front door, I give him a peck on the cheek thank him and quickly walk inside.

I can see johnny standing in the doorway looking dumbfounded for at least five minutes, maybe more, until a customer walks up and assumingly asks him to move so he can enter the store. I quickly clock on and get started.

Chapter 31
Draino

I just dropped Abbigail off to work and I'm speechless. She gave me a peck on the cheek, it was amazing. I feel like I'm walking on clouds the whole way home. I've had so many doubts as to whether she would ever catch feelings for me, that it makes me sigh with relief. Not all hope is lost yet.

School holidays are coming up soon and I'd like to take Abbigail away for the weekend somewhere nice. I spoke to my employment agency and they're paying for my learners and four driving lessons this week coming. Freedom here we come. Pretty exciting shit. I start walking back to my crib, I'll come back later when Abbigail's finished work.

Right now, though I have a learner's test to study for…

Chapter 32
Abbigail

It's getting late and I've just finished work. I look around for Johnny and I can't see him anywhere. I sit at a table on the outside of the restaurant and flick Johnny a quick text. I wait about five or ten minutes then start walking, wondering if maybe he'll meet me along the path somewhere.

It's dark outside and kinda chilly, I wrap my arms around myself and keep walking left, right, left. I put some tunes on from my phone, letting the beat carry me home. I've got my earphones in and suddenly some dodgy looking dude pops out from around the corner. It looks like a knife in his hand, shit. I start talking to myself out loud pretending to talk to Draino on the phone. It's about now I realise I should've caught a cab.

Obviously all of a sudden the fella in the dark hoody dark tracksuit pants and no-name shoes grabs my bag. I try to stop him by pulling hard on the strap still attached to my shoulder; fuck. My phone's in my pocket and just as I'm about to give up and run, I see Johnny running toward me fast as anything. I yell at the top of my voice.

"Draino, he's got a knife."

The fella looks at Draino coming toward him.

"Shit, fucken Draino." I hear him swear under his breath. Suddenly, he lets go of my bag and runs in the opposite direction. OK. I shake my head as my knees start to give way. Johnny catches me as my knees are about to hit the ground.

"Fuck," he says "Abbigail I am so fucking sorry I must have dozed off and I forgot to set the alarm. I woke up and saw your message. I ran as fast as I could. Are you OK?"

"Bit shaken but I'll be OK. Next time I'll catch a cab home but."

"There won't be a next time I promise."

I wrap an arm around Johnny's waist and we start walking the rest of the way back to my unit. We get in the door and I turn to look at Johnny. He looks exhausted and I feel guilty. He's always running around after me and I feel like I'm weak as shit. How is it that the other girls go through life never needing someone to protect them and then; there's me. I don't go looking for trouble. It finds me at every corner. It sucks to be me. I stop and turn around to Johnny and yell at him.

"I'm not your fucking problem, Johnny. There's no reason for you to protect me all the fucking time. Do you think I'm useless? Just some weak bitch who can't look after myself, Johnny, hmmm. You think I'm your problem. Well news flash sunshine, I'm my problem and my responsibility. I don't need you or anyone else to sort my life out for me!"

Johnny looks at me with a sad look on his face. He turns to walk away and then looks back at me.

"I will see you tomorrow, Abbigail. Goodnight."

I growl and start to cry slamming the door behind me after I walk inside.

I'm angry at myself for feeling weak, scared and alone. I'm not holding strong, not today anyway.

I slide down the back of the door and sit on the floor crying. I'm not sure how long I'm there for before I drag myself to bed. A shower can wait till morning as I lay down on top of the bed uniform on and all. It's another day down.

Tomorrow is a new beginning.

Chapter 33

Draino

I'm a broken man as I walk home. I'm glad it's dark and the streets are empty, knowing damn well I can't stop the tears from sliding silently down my cheeks. Fucking hell, now thanks to that street prick Jacko; I'm a broken man. I'll kill him. He better hope he doesn't run into me for a very long time. If I ever, ever, catch him mugging a girl again; I'll break his fucking legs.

Even if it's some other chic and not Abbigail. Like fuck! Where is his respect fucking gone? I hit the power pole as I keep walking. I look at my phone hoping there's a text I've missed from Abbigail; anything to let me know we're sweet. Nothing, damn it!

I walk home with my knuckles now bleeding. Why does life never work out as planned? Abbigail always says we need to hold strong, I've never been so broken.